The Places Between

Terry Grimwood

Pendragon Press

First Published in 2010 by
Pendragon Press
Po Box 12, Maesteg, Mid Glamorgan
South Wales, CF34 0XG, UK

ISBN 978 1906864 20 0

Typeset by Christopher Teague

Printed and bound in Great Britain by
CPI Antony Rowe, Chippenham and Eastbourne

www.pendragonpress.net

For my wife, the lovely Jessica

Chapter One

Rebecca Ann Samuels' journey was a maddened, headlong dash along narrow lanes, where endless hedgerows strobed through the cone of her head-lamps. There was no time. Dawn would be too late.

The big BMW she drove was a cocoon of rich, soft engine growl, unlike her own battered little hatchback. The BMW belonged to her husband, to David –

Mustn't think about Dr David Samuels, she had to concentrate on getting to the woods fast and alive.

Something flew over the car. . .

Caught in the upper edge of the light cone, not a bird, too big, man-sized, Dear God, *man-sized!* Its wings were fleshy, gliding wings. A tail snaked out in its wake. It banked abruptly, and hurtled back at the windscreen, jaws wide, teeth - nothing but teeth - bared.

Rebecca screamed and swerved, there was a nightmare of juddering, then she was thrown back across the road and up against the opposite bank. Branches lashed at the glass, scraped paint.

It stopped, a violent, near-instant, transition from motion to stillness that wrenched her against the seat belt and jerked her skull first forwards, then backwards against the headrest.

There was silence. The headlights no longer lit up a stretch of empty road but a tangle of branches and leaves where the stalled BMW's bonnet had dug itself into the hedge. Perhaps she should call a breakdown service, someone with a tow truck. Then she remembered that she could call no one. She was alone. She closed her eyes, waited for her breathing to steady.

Another memory. The flying thing. Panicked, she unclipped her seat belt and leaned forward to peer up and out of the windscreen. She saw mostly hedge, though there were glimpses of a brightly starred sky.

She wouldn't be able to see it if it came back.

Except it wasn't going to come back, it was never there in the first place. It was a hallucination, perhaps an owl, distorted by her stress-wracked mind – But it had looked so...so demonic, like something sent from Hell to take her rotten soul back to where it belonged.

No! She slammed her fist down onto her thigh. The dull, sudden pain cleared her mind. She twisted the key, the engine purred into life

1

and she thanked a God who had no business helping her at all. She crunched the BMW into reverse. The car rocked, the wheels spun, then she was moving, a short, bumpy stagger back onto the road. She straightened the vehicle, pushed the gear into first, and stopped.

There was something wrong here. She didn't recognise the lane. It was wider than most of the roads around here, and straighter, slicing into the darkness far beyond the range of her headlamps. Rebecca received a sense of immense, almost terrifying distance. The vegetation was wrong too, the hedges, leafless tangles of thorn, the trees, stark and grey-white with smooth multiple trunks that twisted about one another in a grotesquely sensuous embrace. Their foliage was littered with vast flowers.

Something moved, slithered, yes *slithered*, out of the leaf canopy of a tree almost directly to her left. She rammed the car into reverse and it lurched drunkenly backwards until it erupted out onto a fork in the road. She didn't remember the fork. There had only been the lane, the hedges, her cargo…She reversed a few more yards until the BMW's headlamps showed her a familiar narrow stretch bent into a sharp bend about twenty yards ahead.

She glanced left as she resumed her journey, but saw no sign of the entrance to the strange road - no, wait, perhaps a small, night-shadowed gap, perhaps not.

There was no time to worry about it, time was wasting and she had to get to the woods.

Something had flown over the car and then she had seen something else slithering out of a tree that may not have been a tree, but an immense clump of flowers on the side of a road that shouldn't exist…

There were lay-bys at regular intervals along the border of Foxhill wood. Rebecca parked in the third one she came to. She was stiff, bruised from her crash, from the exertions of earlier, from the fear and shock that had tightened her joints and shredded her nerves.

Outside, the night air was warm enough to taste. Rebecca stood for a moment and hugged herself, a tall, frail-seeming woman in her early thirties, with long brown hair, and naturally pale skin. She was wearing a summer dress and an over-large woollen v-neck. Her clothes were stained, with her own sweat, and with other things that had once belonged to David.

An owl hooted, and in the distance, a fox yipped. A full moon silvered the world. Rebecca shivered, then dragged her shattered courage together, hurried round to the boot and opened it.

The courtesy light flicked on and there, crammed into a messy foetal-curl, was Dr David Samuels, GP for the Suffolk Village of Abbotsfield, and husband to Rebecca Ann. He was still dressed in the pink, pin-striped Van-Heusen shirt and matching tie he had been wearing when Rebecca had followed him into the garage, but it was all stained now, with the blood and other ichors that had spilled from his ruined head.

His eyes were open.

Rebecca had never seen a dead person before tonight. She had not been prepared for the odd intelligence, and the resentment, that would remain in a corpse's eyes. She had not been prepared for the stillness, the impossible *absence*, the unthinkable reality that whatever she did or said to that human body, it would no longer respond.

It would not wake up. Ever.

So don't wake up now, she pleaded silently.

She glanced upward, an instinctive action. There was darkness, there were stars.

No flying thing, nothing that slithered...

Then it was back to her night's work, which she could *not* complete, because she could not *touch* him again. But she had touched him before, had got him into the car, so she *could* touch him again, couldn't she? She hesitated though, because dead flesh was substance only, like meat. And it was that pure-fleshness that made her stomach cramp and her skin crawl.

Oh for God's sake! She reached in abruptly, and grabbed his legs and yanked them, with much grunting and straining, over the edge of the boot. She grabbed his belt. There was more heaving, a grotesquely ludicrous battle with a life-size, life-less man-thing. Rebecca had used the hoist in David's garage to put him into the boot. There was no hoist out here.

A pause for breath preceded another immense effort; arm, shirt, belt, leg, followed by a teetering that could have gone either way. It went her way and she yelped and jumped back as David flopped against her, hands clawing, head nodding, and crashed to the ground at, and on, her feet.

Dragging came next. She had already done this, but that had been on a smooth concrete floor. This haul was through bracken, over uneven, loamy earth, over fallen boughs and roots. This dragging was slow and stabbed pain into her back and fire into her arms. She kept going, though, stumbling and tripping as she struggled backwards into the wood.

She didn't know where she was headed, but she knew the right spot when she found it; a small patch of bare earth, felt rather than seen in the tree-obscured moonlight. She dropped David's legs, leaned against the nearest tree for a moment, then set off back to the car to fetch a spade and a torch.

Her footfalls were soft thuds and rustles. The sounds grew around her. Her footsteps, *his* footsteps. Behind her. David. She increased her pace, refusing to look round. David was coming for her, all bloody and angry and wanting revenge.

She spun round, and there was nothing but moon-painted forest.

Returning to the corpse was worse. David would be gone, would have got up and walked away, was, hiding, waiting...

But he was, just as she had left him. In a way that was even more terrible, because it was a confirmation of this new and horrible reality.

Rebecca drove the shovel into the peaty woodland floor. There was a dull thud of steel on springy earth. She worked hard, pausing only occasionally to wipe sweat from her forehead using a woollen sleeve stiffened with blood and dirt.

Sheet lightning illuminated the slivers of horizon visible through the gaps in the trees. Thunder grumbled, God probably. She had never stopped believing in Him or His righteous indignation, which she had learned to fear in the Baptist Chapel she had attended until she had married –

- *this* man, lying here.

Something flew over her.

She snapped her head up, caught a glimpse of...of what? A shadow, a movement, outstretched, gliding wings? She peered into the dark, and saw nothing.

More important than imagined devils, was the question of how deep the grave must be to hide the sac of meat, bones and vitals that had been her husband, and to keep him safe from the nostrils of hungry foxes, crows and dogs.

Lightning, a flicker of blue white that unveiled the patiently waiting shape, sprawled where Rebecca had dumped it. Thunder rumbled. She cried. And thrashed the shovel's blade into the ground, scraped and levered and lifted and poured, back bent, arms beyond aching. A gust of damp, chilled wind forced its way through the wood. Branches hissed, trunks groaned.

She couldn't get away with this. She was doomed. Oh God... no, mustn't take His name in vain, because He was coming, rolling steadily across the sky, closing in, dark and vengeful and so very, very angry –

She glanced round wildly at the imprisoning bars of the conifers, dark against the dark, then, momentarily visible as lightning licked the sky.

In that moment she saw, between the tree trunks, other, different plants; fleshy stemmed, thorny stemmed, huge leaves, titanic and startling blooms. Worse, the vegetation was astir; things crept and slid and scuttled.

That Place again.

Hell perhaps? It was where she belonged wasn't it?

A Place full of things that crept and slithered and scuttled (and flew?), heading in this *direction, coming for her...*

She threw her shovel to the ground, grabbed her husband's ankles for one last time and dragged him to the hole she had made for him. It was a good fit. Lightning displayed her work in all its awful splendour; the ragged slot carved into the earth, and David's body, on its side, face shoved into the rough wall of his grave.

David...

Grief ripped through her. Poor David, her husband, her lover. This was all her fault. She had misunderstood him, failed him...

She let herself cry, unable to stem the rage of convulsive, gagging sobs until it eased enough for her to return to the task of closing the grave. It began to rain, a widely spaced spatter of heavy, warm drops. She worked on until she had covered her husband in loamy soil, patting it down with the flat of the shovel.

I'm sorry, I'm sorry, I'm sorry...

Then she ran, resolve broken, feeling the entire weight of the demon-glutted darkness rear up behind her. She tripped, scrambled back to her feet, oblivious to the bruising shock of her fall, lurched on, fell again.

Coming, Oh God, they were coming out of that Place...

Chapter Two

She woke.

And sat up in bed, head pounding, choking on panic, trying not to remember, to make it a dream.

Oh God she had …

… covered her tracks, that's what, cleaned and swept until dawn. Exhausted yet wide awake, she had scoured the garage and then the house until satisfied that every vestige of David was gone. All that remained was a black bin liner, tied tight on its cargo of bloodied evidence and waiting in the garage to be delivered to the nearest landfill site.

It was already hot, the sun-drenched bedroom stifling. Rebecca grabbed her robe, which hung on the back of the door, and forced herself downstairs, inspecting the floor as she went, looking for blood stains, hairs, other forensic evidence.

They *would* find it, molecules of David that had escaped the vacuum cleaner and 1001.

David had not come home, that's what she would tell the police if (when) they came for her. No, that wouldn't work, his car was there. He *had* come home then walked out, yes, walked out. Oh God, she couldn't think. The phone rang.

Rebecca's breath snagged in her throat.

She didn't have to answer.

But it wouldn't stop. On and bloody on it went, insisting that she run downstairs and pick up the receiver. Now Rebecca, now, now, *now!*

"Rebecca?" It was Lynne.

No words came, none even formed in her mind.

"Rebecca? Are you still there? Are you alright?"

"Yuh…yes."

"Has he hit you again?"

The confession had burst out of her last night, before she had come home to find David, sitting in the armchair, *that* armchair over there. He had been furiously silent. Shaking his head, he had stood up, very deliberately, pushed past her and headed for the kitchen where there was a side door into the garage. He liked her to be there when he came home, demanded it of her.

Normally she would have apologised.

Normally.

"No," she heard herself answer. "I'm...I've got a migraine." That wasn't a lie.

"Are you sure?"

"I need to go back to bed."

"I'm coming round to see you."

"Please don't Lynne - "

"He *has* hit you hasn't he. You can't let him get away with this."

"It's okay. Please Lynne. I just need to get some sleep."

"I'm not so sure -"

Rebecca hung up and winced. The oncoming headache was going to be a bad one.

There would be no rest until the trip to the dump was over with. She should do it now, before her head got worse. Back upstairs, she washed quickly, brushed her hair then returned to the bedroom and opened the wardrobe door.

To David's clothes.

Clothes, holding a person's scent and even shape within their dead material, *his* sweat, *his* aftershave, *him*...Shuddering at their touch, Rebecca reached inside to withdraw a loose fitting, sleeveless white blouse and ankle-length skirt. The clothes swung back to fill the gap her arm had made, sleeves flapped accusingly.

The dump was a sun-baked, foul-smelling quadrangle, walled by ranks of giant skips, each one accessible via a set of metal steps.

Rebecca dragged the bin liner up the nearest set. The bag was heavy, because it contained, among other things, her jumper and summer dress, a spade and a claw hammer. Getting it into the skip would be difficult, because the lip was a good five feet from the platform. She hauled the bag up to stomach height. Her arms shook, her head throbbed.

"Here, let me help."

Startled, she spun round to see a grinning, middle-aged Good Samaritan complete with greying DA and cup-sleeved tee shirt.

Rebecca mumbled a thank you. He took the bag. "Bloody hell love," he growled. "You got a body in here?" With a grunt he hefted it into the skip where it tumbled into the chaos of discarded furniture, garden refuse and broken toys.

Elvis sang "Heartbreak Hotel" loudly as the Good Samaritan drove away.

Rebecca studied her clothes before getting back into her own, oven hot Fiesta. The blouse was still bright white, the skirt unruffled. She slid behind the wheel, closed her eyes for a moment against the rhythmic sledgehammer inside her skull, then started the engine and headed home.

Where Lynne Taylor was waiting, leaning against her Mini's nearside door, arms folded.

"I was worried," she said.

The deeply tanned Lynne wore a sleeveless lilac top and a short skirt. Lynne was always well-dressed, determinably divorced and defiantly single. She was also the best friend Rebecca had ever known.

"Sent you out shopping, did he, even with a migraine?"

"No," Rebecca answered quietly.

"Come on, let's go indoors. I'll make you a coffee."

Rebecca was grateful enough to cry.

"David's not here," Lynne observed, a few minutes later, as she placed a tray laden with mugs of coffee and a packet of biscuits onto the low table beside the sofa.

"He's left me."

"My God Rebecca. When was this?"

"Last night. There was note. I found it when I got back from yours."

"Where's he gone? His car's still on the drive."

Rebecca shrugged. "I don't know."

"Has he taken anything?"

"No." Dear God, listen to her lies. "He must have come home, left the note and walked out."

Lynne shook her head. "The bastard. Look, you do realise that he might have gone off with someone else, don't you. I don't mean to be cruel but it is a possibility."

"I did wonder."

"There is another possibility..." Lynne put her mug on the table, reached out and lay her hand on Rebecca's.

"Another?"

"Well, yes. He could be dead."

"Dead?"

"Hey, Rebecca I didn't mean to frighten you. It's just that, well, he's left all his clothes, his car...I'm sorry to be so blunt, but you have to prepare yourself for the worst."

"I hadn't thought of that," Rebecca murmured. She wanted Lynne to go away. She wanted to be alone. She wanted to go to bed, close her eyes and hide.

"Have you got the note?"

"Note? Uh…no. I threw it away. I wasn't thinking."

"It's alright Rebecca. I'm sure I'm wrong. But perhaps this is for the best. He was hurting you. You're better off without him." She frowned. "You realise that he'll probably be back for his things. You'll have to be strong. Call me if you need me."

Rebecca nodded again, another painful movement of her head.

"Look, I'm supposed to be having lunch with some friends." Lynne was drawing a mobile phone from her handbag. "I'll make my excuses -"

"No, I'm okay. Really."

"Are you sure? You look terrible."

"I want to be on my own."

There was silence after Lynne left, silence and the deep, dense pulse of the blood vessels in her temples. The silence sang all around her, drove her upstairs, where, later, she screamed herself awake, spilling the duvet onto the floor and staring wildly about the room. She could taste him, David, on her lips, in her mouth. His kisses were gritty with soil.

Breathing hard, she looked at the clock; it was just after three in the afternoon. A motorcycle hammered passed. Her head still ached.

The silence returned. No one had found David yet. No one knew he was gone. Even the police seemed blissfully unaware.

But she *had* lifted that hammer high and brought it down in a vicious, angry, screaming arc –

Out, now! She swung her legs off the bed. God, how she needed paracetomol. There was none in the house.

Ah, now she had an errand, a purpose, a reason to get out and walk.

Abbotsfield village was about a mile away, at the end of a high-hedged lane. Glimpsed through gateways, were fields of golden, wind-rippled corn. Cloud was building, white along the distant borders of the otherwise flawless blue sky.

It was alright, out here, alone.

A gust of warm air plucked at her skirt. An aeroplane droned overhead.

She reached the first houses of the village; a small estate of red-brick council semis where squealing children fought with water pistols and an old man in his shirt sleeves mowed a lawn. She passed the war memorial, then the Baptist Chapel she had been brought up to attend. "Believe in the Lord Jesus Christ and you will be saved," declared its notice board via a lurid orange poster. A Happy Shopper stood a few doors down from the chapel.

The shop's door was wedged open against the stifling heat. The interior was dark, a shelf-lined coffin, a fang-jawed trap. Rebecca froze on the threshold. There were people inside. They might want to talk to her. And they would know, oh it wouldn't take long; one look at her face was all they would need.

She backed out, moved to the window and pretended to study the goods on display.

The glass was a parallel universe inhabited by a pale, gauche woman, bag over her shoulder, and rubbing her arms even though she wasn't cold. Behind her was the ghost of Abbotsfield's Tudor Guild Hall, a scattering of people.

David.

She uttered a loud cry and spun round.

To see him dart away across the road, his clothes unfamiliar, but David nonetheless. Rebecca fell back against the shop front, doubled over, gagging with shock.

People stared.

Still gasping for oxygen, Rebecca fled.

The breeze had strengthened, but was far from refreshing. The sky darkened.

She had seen David…

Of course she had. She would see him again and again. It was only a matter of time before it all came crashing in on her.

Thunder grumbled.

Crushing her fears, she concentrated on the lane, the butterflies and birds, the wind-waved fields, the approaching indigo clouds, their summits flattened into menacing anvil shapes.

"Rebecca."

She froze, heart beating hard, afraid to look back, then walked on, fists clenched, palms damp and hot.

"Rebecca."

Louder this time, and a sense of someone coming, fast.

She turned.

To see.

A distant figure, running towards her along the lane, dark hair tousled, and those clothes again, rough-spun, open-necked shirt, tight trousers, bare feet.

Stifling a cry, she broke into a breathless shamble of her own. Another backward glance revealed that he was gaining on her. He... *him*... David.

A sharp pain stabbed Rebecca's side. She was sure he was just behind her, reaching for her, hands dirty with grave-soil, ruined head leaking blood and brain.

A car horn snatched Rebecca's attention back to the road just as an estate swung round the bend in front of her. She threw herself to the left and crashed into the bank where she landed on her side in grass and nettles.

The car surged past, a flash of rust-blotched silver and blast of heavy metal.

And the lane was empty but for diminishing engine-roar. David, or whatever, whoever, she thought was David, had gone. She sat up, trembling, nettle stung and bruised.

Thunder hammered across the darkening sky. The breeze strengthened.

Rebecca ran for home.

Its doors tight shut and locked, its windows bolted, the cottage was a stifling prison. The television roared in the lounge, the radio in the kitchen, providing noise and normality. Rebecca paced, glanced at the telephone, wanting to call Lynne...but no, how could she help?

Lightning flashed bright outside, followed five seconds later by a basso rumble that seemed to go on for hours. Rebecca didn't look at the clock. She didn't want to know the moment David had been twenty-four hours dead.

If he *was* dead.

The thought slipped in quietly. She glanced at the window. The curtains were open and closing them required a huge effort. The driveway, the front garden were places of moving shadow.

Perhaps David had regained consciousness and clawed his way out of his shallow grave?

A movement, fleeting, another.

Something had flown over the car...

Lightning.

And figures, apelike, hurrying across the lane towards the house, naked, their flesh bruise-coloured and hairless. Their heads were huge, their torsos ridiculously small, their arms and legs ludicrously long and thin. Their hands were claws. They were the surreal insanities, nightmares made flesh.

They froze, ran again, dissolved into shadow…

There had been a Place, where the flowers were trees and things slithered…

Rebecca wrenched the curtains closed then snatched up the telephone and, for a moment, was tempted to punch in nine-nine-nine. An ansafone clicked in.

"Lynne, please call me…"

She ran for the bedroom and foetus-curled on the bed. The curtains were open. She should shut them but she couldn't move.

David was out there.

His hair, unkempt instead of neatly combed, his eyes wild and fevered, as he stood on the gravel driveway, looking up at the bedroom –

She saw him at the window - the upstairs window - silhouetted in lightning.

First Intermezzo

One December afternoon, when she was sixteen, Rebecca was seated at a battered second hand desk in a plywood box above the pig sties at Redwood Farm. The box was called the Office. The only other furniture was a second-hand filing cabinet and the second-hand chair on which she sat.

Rebecca had managed some good O-Level results and this job was a stop-gap until she found herself a career. The stop-gap was becoming permanent, however, due to a debilitating shyness and lack of confidence at interviews.

So, four months after leaving school she was still working in the Office above the pig sties. The job was tedious, and lonely - although she could cope with loneliness, she was used to it.

On that day, like any other, she typed, filed and clock-watched. The air stayed cold, despite the Calor Gas stove, and forced her to keep her coat on. Then, as the light seeping through the grubby window dissolved from grey to black, the Dread began.

The Dread slithered into her at the end of every day. The Dread was Jim Bayfield, her boss. It was when he came up to see her, and said things. They were only words, little flatteries, but they concealed something darker, wickedly exciting, yet terrifying.

Rebecca glanced at her watch. Five-thirty, finish this letter and she could go home. She tapped keys, sipped lukewarm coffee.

Boots tattooed on the wooden stairs outside. The sound made her want to cry.

"Hello Becky," Bayfield said as he came in.

He was stocky, broad, and blue-eyed, with a shock of dusty blonde hair. Tonight, as always, he wore the requisite Barbour coat, heavy sweater and Wellingtons. His accent was upper-class correct, his tone authoritative, but never arrogant or aggressive. There was a blurred edge to it tonight, and a flavour to his breath.

Alcohol.

Rebecca attempted a smile because she had been brought up to be polite. And besides, her father was a builder and relied on the local farmers for work, so the last thing she must do was annoy any of them.

Bayfield moved to the window and stared out into the dark. "What are you doing over the weekend then Becky?"

She would probably stay at home, unwanted by any of the teenage cliques in the village. "I've got nothing planned."

"I can't believe that," Bayfield smiled. "The local lads must be queuing up to take you out."

She felt her cheeks burn. Go away, please, she begged him silently. Please go away and let me go home.

But he wasn't going away. Instead he perched himself on the desk. "Don't know what they're missing, the silly buggers."

There was a pause. Downstairs, the pigs squealed.

"You know Becky. " How she hated being called Becky. "I don't think you have any idea just how attractive you are."

He touched her hair, brushed it gently from her face then trailed his work-roughened fingertips over her cheek, to her lips.

"I can't stop thinking about you," he said, serious now. Rebecca was afraid. He had never been this direct before, innuendos yes, but not this. "My wife...well, it isn't easy between us you see. It's why she's gone away for a few days."

Rebecca wanted him to take his hands from her face. She wanted his eyes off her, out of her.

"Becky..." He shook his head, as if mocking his own foolishness, then, suddenly, took her face in his hands and kissed her. Stunned, she opened her mouth to him and it was a warm, exciting thing. Then she panicked and tore herself away. The chair tipped back, and Rebecca crashed down with it.

"What the hell's the matter with you?" Bayfield snapped, jumping to his feet. Abruptly, irritation became panic. "Oh Christ, I'm sorry."

He reached for her again. Rebecca scuttled backwards, her own legs tangled in the chair legs. "Becky," he shouted. "For fuck's sake try to under -"

Rebecca clawed her nails through the hard flesh on the back of his hands. He snatched them back, swore then slapped her. The blow slammed through Rebecca's skull, a moment of white shock, followed by the sting of tears and Bayfield's drunken, contrite gibbering. Rebecca lunged for the door.

She clattered down the plywood stairs and out into the floodlit farmyard. Her bicycle was leaning against the barn wall. Rebecca grabbed the handlebars, made to climb on.

Bayfield erupted out of the barn. Adrenaline-fired, Rebecca swung the bike round and threw it. There was a chaos of flailing limbs and spoked wheels. Rebecca pounded towards the main gate. Beyond lay a long driveway leading to the road.

Footfalls thudded across the yard behind her, each one driving a fist of raw panic into her abdomen. She reached the gate, planted one foot on the bottom bar –

Bayfield's arms were strong and brutal. The pain was brief, however, obliterated by an animal terror that kicked her into a frantic thrash of claws and teeth.

Then came the hard, cold ground, and Bayfield's dark weight as he dropped onto her and the tearing began.

And stopped.

Bayfield stumbled back. "Oh shit," he groaned. "Christ..."

Wet and mud-smeared, Rebecca struggled to her feet.

"Go home" Bayfield was breathing hard. "It was a mistake, that's all. I'm sorry. Here, let me help." He wheeled her bicycle across the yard and handed it to her. "Forget about it eh?" he said. "These things happen. No harm done."

Rebecca called at the village police house on the way home. PC Copes, cold-eyed and hatchet-faced, was out of uniform and dragged from his evening meal by her visit. Later that night, after spending an hour at Redwood Farm, Copes cautioned Rebecca for wasting police time. Rebecca's mother stared in anguished disbelief and her father paced, appalled by the potential loss of a customer and damage to his standing as a chapel elder.

Chapter Three

Hugging a thick black zip-up cardigan about herself against the early Sunday morning chill, Rebecca left her car in the third lay-by and walked once more into Foxhill woods. The night storms had sucked the oven-like heat from the air. There had been rain.

She knew that she was a living cliché; the criminal returning to the scene of her crime, but she needed to know that the David she had glimpsed in the village, who had followed her along the lane, who had pounded at the bedroom window last night, was a David from her guilt-fevered sub-conscious and not the one she had buried, here, in these woods.

She followed a trail of crushed bracken that looked as if something had recently been dragged through it. Rebecca's mouth dried, her pulse accelerated. Something *had* been dragged through the bracken hadn't it? Wet vegetation quickly soaked the lower half of her jeans. A rabbit broke cover and darted across her path. Birds sang.

And there it was, much closer to the road than she had remembered it to be, a clearly discernable mound of freshly turned earth. All it needed was a headstone, a name, an accusation.

So, was she disappointed, relieved, or more afraid because this meant that her mind really was fraying at the seams? She didn't know. All she felt was confusion. *She* had done this. Rebecca Ann Samuels, respectable and respected wife of a respectable and respected GP. Rebecca Samuels who read all the usual books, who watched all the usual television programmes, who knew everyone in the village, who was popular, kind and polite, who never caused a fuss or raised her voice, who was never rude or controversial, who was so unrelentingly normal. She had come to this place in the belly of the night to dig a secret grave for the husband she had beaten to death with a hammer.

She knew she should get away, quickly, before the first dog walkers arrived. But she couldn't. She *had* to stand over it and terrify herself with the enormity of what she had done. A temptation to open the grave overwhelmed her. A thorough check, or was it that she wanted to see him again, all folded up and dirt defiled, perhaps even worm-drilled?

She felt herself move closer, the compulsion arising from some deep and masochistic corner of her mind. It forced her through the remaining undergrowth until she was standing over the grave, which was surrounded by a moat of beaten-down bracken that announced to the world that spade business had recently been conducted in the this spot.

Rebecca sank slowly to her knees.

David...She reached out, flinched back, then driven by some need she could not comprehend, lay the fingertips of her right hand on the soil. It was cold and damp. It must be even colder and damper below, inside.

She pushed her fingers into the earth.

Are you there David? Are you reaching back towards me? Will you touch me? He was stirring, she could see it, vivid on the blood-splashed viewing screen in her head. He was twisting over in his stifling, earth-clogged bed, driving his own hand up, up, brushing his cold, cold fingertips against hers -

She reared backwards and dropped onto her bottom in the wet, crushed bracken. Dear God, what the hell was she doing? This place was dangerous. She had to get away, *now*. But she couldn't move. The small mound of soil held her. He's here, in there.

She scrambled to her feet, then turned and walked quickly away. She wanted to look over her shoulder, to check he wasn't clawing his way to freedom. Her breathing was shallow, ragged, her mind surged with raw and primal fear. She stared at the forest floor, afraid of tripping, trying to find the corpse-formed path. It was here, somewhere, it had to be. The sense of dread increased, and with it, the panic-anger. She should return to the grave, trace the path from there.

Oh no, she could not, could never, do that.

The bracken thinned, and then cleared altogether.

Rebecca stumbled to a halt.

And when saw where she was, she wanted to scream. She stayed silent, however. Screaming wouldn't help. Thinking might, but not screaming.

She was in that *Place* again, the one she had driven into by accident the other night – *that* night – and later had glimpsed between the tree trunks while digging David's grave.

She glanced round, hoping to find the other woods, the woods in *her* world. But there was nothing, only a wide path, those huge flowers, and titanic trees that blotted out the sky. She deserved this didn't she, deserved to be trapped in this lush porchway into Hell?

A huge, translucent, slug-like creature broke through the undergrowth to her left.

Rebecca stared, transfixed by its physicality, by the ripple of membranous flesh, the restless probing of eye-stalks. She saw its vitals, the flow of life-fluid through the vessels that latticed its flesh.

And the faces of the people trapped inside its body, faces pressed against see-through skin, mouths open, eyes wide with the madness of the damned.

There was a loud, wet crash. Rebecca spun about to see another of the creatures slide onto the path behind her. Another crash and there were three of them, closing in from all sides.

The nearest creature's head swung towards her. Its mouth opened; a splitting of slime-wetted flesh. Voices howled from its maw, the sounds devoid of sanity.

Beyond it were familiar trees, the shores of the bracken sea, Oh God, safety, except that Rebecca's escape route was a gap between the creature and the border of the alien forest. She had no choice; it was run or die - or was it run *and* die? Concentrating on the gap, and only the gap, Rebecca drove herself into a desperate, bent-double sprint.

The world became a wide-open maw…Then she was careering along the monster's flanks.

A prehensile tongue snapped the air just behind her head. The shock unbalanced her into a collision with the huge stem of one of the flowers.

She recovered and ran, back muscles tensed, waiting for the lash of that tongue. She focussed on the fir trees ahead, only the fir trees, not wanting to look at the faces beside her, the sanity-devoid eyes, the open, screaming mouths, the hands clawing their translucent prison walls. She didn't want to look, but she did, gut horror made her do it.

They were p, but what sort of p? She glimpsed wings, horns, tails, animal heads…

Past now, with open track in front of her, coniferous forest ahead.

A dog barked.

Rebecca looked back. The slug was still in pursuit, still within tongue-range. Rebecca surged into bracken, grabbed at the nearest tree trunk and slumped against it, out of breath, chest on fire. She glanced round wildly and caught a glimpse of a wide track, huge flowers, and unnameable beasts. Then all of it was gone. Hallucination over.

The barking grew frantic. A human voice snapped angrily but the dog wasn't listening.

Rebecca choose a direction and walked. She was lucky and in a few minutes, saw her car. Another car, the dog walker's she supposed, was parked in front of it. A grey-haired woman sat in the passenger seat, reading a newspaper. She looked up as Rebecca passed by and said "Good morning," through the open window.

Rebecca, discreet with her dishevelled hair and sodden clothes, had no choice but to return the greeting.

"Are you alright?" the woman called out as Rebecca fumbled car keys.

"Yes…Yes, I fell over. Stupid…wasn't looking where I was going."

"You look rather shocked. Are you sure you can drive?"

Rebecca nodded. More barking and curses erupted from the woods. The woman glanced into the trees. "Oh dear," she chuckled. "Clive never could control that animal."

As she drove homewards, Rebecca met a police car. It startled her into a wild swerve as it was hurled round a blind bend and into her path. Blue light flashed, headlamps glared and displaced air rocked Rebecca's Fiesta. Shaken, she swung into a field gateway to wait for the trembling to stop.

Did Police car equal discovered corpse, no doubt sniffed out by Clive's disobedient canine? Oh God… The shaking grew worse. It could be over soon. All she had to do was turn the car about, follow the police back to their destination.

If they had found David, it would only be a only a matter of time before they knew that the deceased's wife was Rebecca Samuels nee Wright. *That* Rebecca Wright, the police time-waster.

A second police car hurtled by.

Later, Rebecca pushed her un-powered Ransome back and forth across the lawn at the back of her cottage. She preferred the push mower. Petrol mowers were too noisy and she was nervous of the trailing leads that powered an electric version.

She had to keep moving, lost in the tick-tick-tick of the mower as she waited, for the hue and cry and the wail of sirens.

"Rebecca!"

She started and spun round, breath snagged in her throat. Why did everyone want to take her by surprise?

It was Lynne, neat, sharp and crisp as ever, standing by the patio doors. "I rang the bell, you didn't answer." She hurried across the newly mowed lawn, her progress hampered by tight skirt and heels. "I picked up your message on my answer phone." She sounded breathless. "I came as soon as I could."

19

Rebecca shook her head, still unable to frame any words then set off once more into the remaining long grass. She sensed Lynne hurrying to catch up with her.

"He hasn't been back has he?" Lynne shouted above the din of the mower. "He hasn't hit you again?"

She planted herself in Rebecca's path. Rebecca stopped. Why wouldn't Lynne leave her alone? Couldn't she see she was busy?

"God Rebecca, you're as white as a sheet. Look, I'll get my phone and call a doctor."

A doctor? Now that was funny. Robert Miles was the duty GP this weekend. "Yes," she said. "Let's get Robert round here shall we. He'll want to know where David is –

"Just tell him everything."

"Tell him?" Rebecca began to laugh, the sound bubbled uncontrollably from her throat, then turned, abruptly, into tears. "I can't tell him. I can't –"

"Why can't you tell him?" Lynne was gentle, holding Rebecca's arms.

"Because David is dead."

"You can't be certain –"

"He's dead." Rebecca knew she should stop there, but the floodgates were open. "*I* killed him. Me. I killed David." She stumbled into silence, appalled at what he had just done.

"No," Lynne said at last. "No Rebecca. He's left you, or maybe committed suicide. You're just blaming yourself…"

"It wasn't suicide. It wasn't an accident. I hit him and hit him until he was dead."

With the hammer, the one with the pterodactyl head and oil-darkened handle.

There was a seat, shaded by an ancient apple tree. The two women sat side-by-side, staring at the lawn. From the village, the church bell called faithful and sinner. That's where I should be, Rebecca thought. Making my peace with God.

"Tell me, straight," Lynne said. "Did you…Did you really kill David?"

Rebecca told her straight.

"My God. . . You must go to the police. You know that don't you," Lynne said gently.

"I can't."

"They would understand."

Rebecca laughed, the sound bitter. "Would they?"

"You're a beaten wife."

"Where are the bruises Lynne?" She looked directly at her friend. "There are reasons I can't go to the police, why they wouldn't believe me."

"But look at you. You're not going to hold up much longer. You're on the verge of a breakdown." Lynne stood up.

"Oh, you're right there Lynne. You have no idea what's happening to me."

"Rebecca, you were the first person to befriend me in this village and you've turned out to be the best friend I've ever had. So listen to me. I'm going to get my mobile from my bag. We'll phone the police together. I'll stay with you. All the way -"

"No!" Panic drove Rebecca to her feet. "Don't you dare Lynne. No!"

But Lynne was already striding towards the house. Rebecca managed a single, faltering step.

Then froze, as reality side-slipped.

As David emerged from the house.

Chapter Four

"**G**ood morning Lynne," David said pleasantly.

Rebecca forced herself to sit down and not run or scream. David smiled. His eyes were bright, laughing almost.

He carried a tray laden with tea-making accessories and wore a denim shirt, tucked neatly into a pair of fawn Chinos. Familiar clothes, though never worn as well as they were worn today.

And then he was close, carefully placing the tray on the seat beside her. She smelled his aftershave, the faint detergent scent of his clothes, and the shampoo in his hair. She saw his skin, its texture, colour, the lines – fewer perhaps, as if there had been a lessening of life's tension.

"It's alright Rebecca," he said quietly. "Don't be afraid."

He walked back towards the house, past Lynne and indoors. Rebecca felt a need to rush after him, to question and demand and… but the shock was too debilitating.

Lynne stood over her, a return unnoticed by Rebecca. "What's going on?" she said with ominous gentleness.

Rebecca couldn't meet her eyes, let alone speak.

"Is he… Is that bastard messing you up? Is that it Rebecca?"

Messing her up? No…Yes…Perhaps…

"Rebecca? Are you listening to me?"

She supposed she was, she wasn't sure. Nothing was sure anymore.

"I'm sorry, I have to go," Lynne said crisply. "I can't handle this, not right now. Look, I'll call you, later."

Rebecca nodded. When she looked up, Lynne was gone.

Everyone was gone. The garden was empty. The house…

Her nerve failing, Rebecca paused on the threshold of the conservatory that formed the rear entrance to the cottage. She had to go in, now, before her resolve crumbled completely. Swallowing heavily, she stepped through the open doorway. The conservatory was hot, its air hard to swallow.

Blood roared in her head.

She uttered his name.

No answer. It wasn't going to be that easy. There was silence, dense, heavy, empty-house silence.

She moved past the wicker chairs and potted plants and into the kitchen. It too was deserted, but for a solitary fly, bouncing, single-mindedly against the window. Rebecca spoke David's name more loudly, her voice shocking in the quiet. There was no reply.

The lounge was empty. He wasn't here, unless, he was waiting for her upstairs. Perhaps he wanted their reunion to be a complete one. Rebecca shivered.

Another hesitation, this time at the foot of the staircase that swept up to the sunlit landing. Rebecca forced herself onto the bottom step, then on into a slow, wearisome climb, legs aching, joints stiff, clutching at the stair rail like an old woman.

There were choices here…no, only *one* choice. The bedroom, her bedroom, *their* bedroom. The door was ajar. She pushed it gently, then stepped back as it swung open. Images hit her, familiar, frightening. The bed, unmade, yesterday's skirt and blouse crumpled on the floor, the wardrobe doors open.

Open?

She had shut them this morning, unable to bear the sight of his clothes.

Rebecca crossed, reluctantly, to the wardrobe. A tense, cursory inspection revealed that the denim shirt and chinos were missing. There were other empty coat hangers, but she couldn't work out what they had held.

Did ghosts need clothes? Did hallucinations? Even shared hallucinations – Lynne had seen him hadn't she? He was something Lynne "couldn't handle right now".

Rebecca cried. The tears, unexpected and sudden, were not for herself, but for David. The David she had seen just now, the softly-spoken, kind David who told her not to be afraid. It was not the first time he had spoken to her like that. "There is only you Rebecca," he would say in that same quiet voice. She would make him love her then, in those rare, small hours moments. That was when their loving flared bright and true and needed no erotic artifice to stay its course.

Her eyes were closed when David kissed her.

The kiss was deep and warm. The kiss opened her and she pulled him down on top of her. Her hands slid about his back and she felt the hot, dryness of his skin. His weight burrowed into her and she was lost in the dark, alone with David, in her room, deep into the silent hours. She cried as she clawed at him and crushed him down onto and into her. He murmured her name, at first, a whisper, then a moan, a shout.

There's only you Rebecca. . .

A wave gathered, rose and crashed down through her..

Brief moments then, soon lost as the shadows closed once more round his heart.

She wanted them back, no matter the price.

There was a candle, she saw it suddenly, astonished that she hadn't noticed it before. It stood in an ornate candlestick, which was made of something dark, wood-like, but not wood. The stick was twisted into a spiral, tiny symbols engraved into its smooth, shiny surface. The candle itself was white, plain looking. Its flame was blue. Not a hot, gas-flame blue, but cold, icy blue, an unnatural sapphire that Rebecca sensed would freeze rather than burn her skin if she touched it.

The flame was a beautiful thing and she knew that she should not try to extinguish it. It smelled of roses, not the false scent of the gift shop candle, but something harder to pinpoint, as if the fire was the gateway to the flower itself and not the release some wax-bound chemical forgery.

David had left it here, a sign perhaps, reassurance, or simply a gift?

Rebecca sat on the bed and watched it. Her wonder soon palled.

Where were the police? She needed to talk to them. They might listen, they just might. She crossed to the window, looked out. The lane was empty. There were no sirens. Surely they should be here by now. Call them... No, no she couldn't do that.

It was almost two pm. There was a way to find out. She hauled herself to her feet, walked, dazed and limb-heavy, into the kitchen and switched on the radio. She tuned it to a local station. A guitar solo and repeated chorus was fading a current playlist rock song. She leaned on the spotless, light-pine worktop as she waited out another song, then a seemingly endless commercial break. Finally the news erupted out of the tiny speaker. International crisis, political scandal, then...

"Suffolk Police were called out early this morning following the sighting of a bizarre and unidentified creature in Foxhill Woods near Dunwich." There was an edge of sceptical humour in the newscaster's voice. "A dog-walker, whose name has been withheld, claims to have been attacked by a large animal.

"John Smithson spoke to Inspector Andrews of the Suffolk Constabulary."

"At the moment we can't say exactly what happened," said Andrews. "No one has been injured but the gentleman concerned is deeply distressed and has been taken to hospital suffering from shock."

"Is there a possibility it could have been one of the 'Big Cats' sighted in the area over the last few years?"

"We certainly cannot discount the possibility, although the witness certainly did not describe the creature as cat-like. We are searching the area."

"Could it have been a hoax, or hallucination?"

"We are keeping an open mind. We have no reason to doubt that the witness experienced something very unusual and frightening, he is, as I said, very distressed."

The news bulletin was replaced by a weather report.

Rebecca stared blindly at the radio then went outside because she couldn't think of anything else to do. The mower was where she had left it. She grabbed its handle and heaved it into motion.

The police didn't come. Why should they? No one had found a body.

Rebecca was alone all afternoon. She finished mowing, then trimmed the edges and weeded borders until she found herself at the furthest point from the cottage. The garden was 150 feet long. The cottage seemed a long way away.

The light changed from yellow to gold. She was astounded to realise that it was evening now. She had been working for, what, six hours? She had not eaten, or drank. The air was chilled, as it had been this morning. The grass was cold under her knees. She should go indoors.

And then what? Sit and worry? Watch television, pretend nothing had happened. She looked up and saw the high privet hedge bordering the bottom of the garden. Beyond, there was a wheat field and beyond that, more fields and then the village. You could hear the church bells from here; they must have rung already because it felt as if it was well past evensong. The Baptists, her mother and father among them, would be at worship too, settling down for one of Pastor Emerson's hour long sermons or thundering through a hymn.

Oh God, she had forgotten that she had a family, that she was connected in any way to the world out there. Suddenly she wanted them. Perhaps she should go now, wait outside the chapel until they came out, or, better still, go inside and see if God could find it in His heart to forgive her, to make things right, to perform a miracle.

Hadn't He done that already?

Or was it the Devil's tricks? Or was this Hell and she didn't know it yet? Or was she going utterly, completely and irredeemably insane?

Something moved on the other side of the hedge.

More noises; snuffles, a short grunt, a low growl, all merging with the hiss of breeze-troubled corn. She struggled to her feet, stood before the hedge, gardening trowel in her hand. There were several of them, scurrying back and forth beyond the hedge. Looking for a gap, that's what they were doing. Then they would come for her.

There was a violent rustling, a tearing, and the hedge was ripped apart.

A creature erupted out of the gap. Long-armed, small bodied, its head, a mass of eyes and wide-open, fang-lined jaws. It exploded into her world and filled her universe.

For that moment, that fragment of a second, she saw her attacker full on, arms swinging in to take her, mouth wide to devour her. She saw its bloated, undulating tongue, she saw the ridges that arched its mouth, she smelled its raw-meat stink, she saw hairless, bruise-coloured flesh.

It hit her, a detonation of speed and energy that knocked her backwards. The ground slammed into her spine and that was when the panic broke. The world was full of screaming, her own and the creature's. She rolled onto her side and watched the animal writhe and convulse in agony as it was engulfed in oily, smoke-rich flame.

The stench of its death was terrible.

In moments it was a crisped, blackened ruin, then ash, picked up and scattered, red-glowing, by the breeze. Then there was nothing at all. Seconds, minutes, hours? It was hard to tell, but it was gone, consumed by the flame.

She heard squeals and shrieks. She glanced towards the hedge and saw silhouettes scurry back and forth beyond the torn branches. The noises sounded like grief. She sat up, knowing she should get away as quickly as possible, but realising that no more of the monsters were going to cross whatever barrier was protecting her.

Because that was what it was, wasn't it? A... a force field, an invisible fence.

She remembered the candle.

"David?" she murmured. Oh God, this was beyond insanity.

Chapter Five

"**R**ebecca?" said Mary Samuels, David's mother. "Rebecca? Rebecca?" There was a muffled sound, a hand clamped over the mouthpiece Rebecca presumed, then a distant. "Something wrong with the phone dear." The "dear" would be Mary's husband?

"No," Rebecca heard herself say. "No, I'm here."

"Why ever didn't you answer straight away?" There were always questions with Mary Samuels.

"I …"

"Never mind. Look, we're coming to stay for a few days."

No, you're not. You can't. Oh God, you can't come here, now…"I see," she managed.

"We'll arrive tomorrow afternoon. David's got a few days off I believe."

Oh yes, Rebecca replied silently. Lots of days off. Absent without leave they call it in the army. In fact, I'm expecting the surgery to call at any moment to ask me why he hasn't turned up for the Monday morning clinic. I was hoping to be gone before they did.

"… I've already phoned David to see if it's alright with him."

You've *phoned* him? You've phoned *David*?

"At the surgery," Mary said impatiently. "Just now."

Rebecca started, realising that she must have verbalised her shock.

"He said we could contact him there at any time." Mary sounded defensive now. "Rebecca? Rebecca are you there? Oh dear, what *is* going on?"

"I'm sorry, I've got a bit of a headache."

"Another those migraines Rebecca? You really should go to a doctor. I'm, surprised David hasn't sorted them out for you. I'll have a word when I see him."

"Thanks. Yes… thanks."

"You sound as if you ought to go back to bed and get some sleep." She needed to do that alright, she had barely slept all night. You can't sleep very well when your house is besieged by demons and there is a possibility that your dead husband might come to visit at any moment. He's in the habit of doing that you know, Mary, except that it appears that he's had to go to work this morning before he can resume haunting me.

Mary was still talking, about arrival times and an instruction that

Rebecca didn't put herself out too much and an offer to bring a pie or a cake or something. Then she said goodbye and hung up. Rebecca ran upstairs. There was an open suitcase on the bed, half-filled and surrounded by clothes and possessions. She was leaving today. She was running away, not sure where she was going, but escaping nonetheless.

But first…

She grabbed a dress from the case and pulled it on before she realised what she was doing, then she picked up the car keys and headed for the front door.

The surgery was a new, fresh painted, single story building that blended into its backdrop of densely packed trees with a modesty that seemed almost bashful. Yesterday's refreshing breeze had persisted and chilled the air enough for Rebecca to wish that she had brought something to cover her bare shoulders. She also realised that she had not brushed her hair. She made a quick attempt to arrange the mess with her fingers.

Tina, today's receptionist smiled brightly at Rebecca who took a deep, steadying breath, cleared her throat and through a forced smile of her own, said; "I wonder if I could get a message to Dave – Dr Samuels."

Tina's smiled broadened and grew, if that was possible, even whiter and brighter. "Of course you can Mrs Samuels. He's expecting you. I'll tell him you're here."

Expecting her? "It's alright, I can wait until he's finished –"

But it was too late. Conscious of the sudden increase in resentment in the hot, airless waiting room, Rebecca perched herself on the nearest chair. The room was crowded. Some of these people had been here for a long time. Who was she to come barging in on some silly errand to her husband? A fan whirred, but it was fighting a losing battle against the lethargic mass of stale air trapped in the room. Someone said hello Mrs Samuels. Rebecca turned to see a young mother she recognised. She was struggling with a restless toddler and looked hot and harassed.

"He's having a jab today," said the mother, whose name Rebecca couldn't remember. "I don't think he's going to be very happy about that." She laughed nervously. Rebecca managed to return the laugh and a mumbled reassurance that she was sure he would be okay.

What did she know? She was not a mother. David had not wanted children.

Tina spoke into the intercom, then she turned to Rebecca and said "Dr Samuels says that you can pop in as soon as his current patient is finished."

"It's alright. I didn't mean to…"

But Tina was taking another call. Rebecca glanced uneasily at the waiting patients. There were a number of familiar faces, several frowns, but a few smiles of recognition as well. She picked up a magazine and stared blankly at the glossed pages.

The buzzer startled her. She looked up to see the light glowing beside Dr D Samuels. She hesitated; Dr D Samuels. David Samuels. David. Swallowing hard, she hurried out of the waiting room.

There were four doors in the passage, three named for the doctors waiting inside, one for the practice nurse. As Rebecca hesitated, relieved to be away from the claustrophobic press of human beings in the waiting room, the door to David's room opened. She flinched, waiting for him to emerge. He didn't, it was a woman, silver-haired Mrs Ethridge in fact, supported by her ancient husband. Mrs Ethridge was crying, but when she saw Rebecca, the crumpled lines of emotion changed to a smile of unnerving radiance.

"He's cured me," she said. "Your husband, he's cured me, my back…"

"Now come along Elizabeth, you're overwrought."

"I'm not overwrought Tom, you saw what he did."

"Yes, yes, of course. Let's get home shall we, have a nice cup of tea." Tom manoeuvred his wife towards the exit. "I'm sorry Mrs Samuels, Elizabeth gets a bit… you know."

But Elizabeth was not to be silenced easily. "Let go of my arm dear," she said firmly. "I'm not a bit anything." She broke away from the anxious Tom. "It's true." The tears were back. "He *has* healed me. He asked me where it hurt, and then touched me and…To be out of pain, oh to be out of…" Her emotion gained the upper hand, and with a final grasp of Rebecca's arm, she hurried off to rejoin her husband.

Without further hesitation, Rebecca crossed to the door labelled Dr Samuels.

The room was cool, and neat. There was a couch, a drawer unit, a desk and two shelves lined with medical text books. The desk was ancient, dark oak with a battered leather surface and was home to a computer and a set of brown folders containing patients' notes.

David sat behind it.

He was wearing a white shirt and tie she recognised.

Clothes were missing from the wardrobe, the denim shirt and chinos, other items...

He smiled, nodded and indicated the chair that faced him. Rebecca moved slowly, struck by the irony of this. Wasn't a consulting room, one in the old surgery, where she had first met him?

David said nothing until she had sat down. Rebecca stared at him looking for a clue, a telltale sign. She saw only the familiar lines and shades and structures. She saw only David.

"Are you okay?" he asked. And it was his voice, though kinder somehow.

Rebecca nodded.

"You don't look it." He spoke with unfamiliar gentleness. "That will be my fault, won't it?"

His fault? She stared at him, uncomprehending. He looked away for a moment. "I've treated you badly Rebecca. I've done things to you that ... Look, ever since Friday night -"

Friday night? Oh God...

" – I've wanted to make amends. You've been so ill, so withdrawn. I was afraid I'd lost you."

Suddenly he was holding her hands and it was the familiar warmth of his skin, *his* skin, she hadn't realised that even skin was individual, that you could recognise the feel of it. "I haven't lost you have I Rebecca?"

She shook her head.

"Will you give me another chance?"

A nod this time.

"I understand if you want me to leave. I'll fetch my things and go quietly."

At last a word broke through. "Friday?"

He frowned, looked away, then back at her. "I lost control... Thank God I managed to stop myself..."

"But... I..." I what? Killed you?

"Look, you're obviously still upset. Perhaps you need time to think."

"Are you David?" she asked, and was astonished at the question.

He seemed unfazed. "Yes I am. But not the David you knew. I will never that man again." His eyes bore into hers. "I will look after you."

She nodded.

"But only if you want me to."

There was a pause, Rebecca's chance to ask all the questions she knew she should ask; about the murder, the Place, the creatures, her own mind...

David lifted her hand to his lips and kissed it lightly. "You'd better go," he said quietly. "Or my patients will stage a revolt."

You're not David, she screamed at him silently. I want you to be, but you're someone - some*thing* – else.

When she walked, she walked fast, a brisk clip out of his consulting room, out of the surgery and to her car. It was alright. She had not killed her husband. He was alive. *Him?* Yes him.

The shock hit her the moment she reached her car. She leaned against the vehicle, head on her arm as her ears sang and the world spun.

Home. Now. So she could hide and sit and think, perhaps make herself a nice cup of tea, and try to remember what she had or had not done. She might even call Lynne at work, to explain that she had been hallucinating. Or she might still run away. Because David was David and would always be David.

The car coughed into life and she drove, too fast. Any sense of reality was dissolving. Her memory of what had happened, so glass-clear, was shattered. The fracture lines distorted the image.

Hedgerows flickered past. Rebecca forced herself to slow down. There were too many blind corners and no room for easy passing. She rounded the last corner, and rammed her foot onto the brake. The car skidded. The car stopped. Rebecca stared out of the windscreen, appalled. She should drive away now. NOW! But they would catch her wouldn't her? The police, who were waiting outside her cottage.

Second Intermezzo

The wedding of Rebecca Ann to Dr David William Samuels had taken place in Abbotsfield Baptist Church on a wet June Saturday afternoon. The small, rectangular building was full, a sea of dark suits and feminine plumage crammed into its highly polished pews. Smiling faces on strained necks watched Rebecca as she slow-marched into the chapel's hot, wood-rich interior. Her father was on her arm, and she could feel his tremors of nervousness. He was proud though, she could feel that too.

As for Rebecca herself, a prisoner bound in white taffeta and lace, she was afraid. Not merely nervous, or overwhelmed, she was rigid with a stark terror that exhausted her beyond the ability to express her fear, or even speak at all. She wasn't afraid of the crowd, rather it was the overwhelming change this ceremony represented. The final blast of the whirlwind of events and emotions that had picked her up and hurled her into this day.

She moved slowly through the chapel, past the familiar and unfamiliar faces. The organist wasn't playing "Here Comes the Bride" but something classical, and not particularly well. The notes tumbled and jarred vaguely, senselessly.

David turned to watch her, impossibly handsome, suit immaculate. He smiled.

And at that moment Rebecca knew than that this was right, that despite having everything wrenched from her hands and worked up into a vast, expensive ritual that meant nothing and seem to extend far beyond the borders of her feelings, that brief, small smile was the focus that drew her back to what she had come here for.

The classical piece groaned to a halt. There was a bout of muffled rustling and coughing. Pastor Michael Emerson smiled his vast and brilliant smile and announced that the first hymn would be Rebecca's favourite, "A Sovereign Protector I Have".

Was it her favourite? She couldn't remember choosing it. There had been a brief discussion about hymns, mostly suggestions, strongly made, by her parents. Now the solemn tune was in progress, thundered out by the Baptist contingent as if sanctity and volume were in direct proportion to each other. She sensed that David's supporters, on the other hand, were not thundering, but frowning at hymn books as they tried to get to grips with the unfamiliar melody.

It started when she had fallen ill. Dr Samuels had been sitting at his desk, preoccupied with writing notes when Rebecca entered the consulting room. His hair was dark and neat, and when he finally looked up at her, she saw that his eyes were kind eyes. She blushed. The reaction astonished her. Neither had spoken, and here she was glowing like a traffic light and feeling so awkward she hardly dared trust herself to sit down.

"And how can I help you?" he asked. His voice was soft, infinitely calm.

He visited her at home a week later, to check up on her progress. Did GPs do that? His predecessor certainly hadn't. The shorter his association with his patients the better he liked it. The thought that she had been singled out, was a new and exciting one to Rebecca. Or was it? Hadn't she been singled out before, by another pillar of this community?

A week after that, there was a phone call, "For you Rebecca," her mother called, hand over the mouthpiece, and a broad smile on her gaunt, brittle features.

Their first date had been a meal, located among the exposed oak beams and gleaming horse brasses in a faux-traditional country pub. Rebecca wore the only good dress she owned and felt old-fashioned. David wore a dark suit and looked overwhelmingly handsome. The beginning was paralysed by Rebecca's nervousness, just as all those job interviews had been. Then, as she stiffly and carefully consumed soup (slurping and splashing to be avoided at all costs), Rebecca said; "I'm a very lonely person." She stopped, appalled at making such a personal confession so early on in…in what, their relationship?

Dr David Samuels stopped eating, returned his spoon to his own bowl of homemade tomato soup and said; "So am I."

The hymn ended, the ritual began. There were coughs, the occasional muted sob, a whisper, a baby-cry, unsuccessfully hushed, then followed by the clip-clop of maternal heels. At the end of it they were finally committed in the eyes of a God Rebecca had lived with all her life yet felt she didn't know very well at all.

Chapter Six

A police patrol car and an unmarked, silver Montego blocked the entrance to Rebecca's drive. Shock-drained, she sat in her hatchback and waited as a uniformed officer sauntered towards her.

"You can't leave your vehicle here I'm afraid," the constable said.

"I live here." Rebecca was surprised at her calm. "And I can't get into my drive."

The constables' eyes widened. "Ah, I see."

He led her past the police car, then past the BMW, to the front door, where a further uniformed officer waited. Off to one side, a man and woman in plain clothes were deep in conversation.

"Excuse me ma'am," Rebecca's officer said. "This lady says she's the owner of the house."

The woman turned and stared at Rebecca. She looked to be in her forties, was tall with dark brown, shoulder-length hair and was introduced, by her ID card, as Detective Chief Inspector Sarah March, Suffolk Constabulary CID.

"I'm Rebecca Samuels."

March regarded her for a moment longer, then said; "I think we'd better go inside."

Rebecca unlocked the front door, the action dreamlike, disconnected from the previous and equally skewed I've-been-let-off-the-hook reality. She led the way into the sitting room where March seated herself in the armchair. The other detective, much younger, in his late twenties perhaps, stood by the door.

"Mrs Samuels, I want to show you something and I want to know if you recognise it." March nodded to her assistant who crossed the room and offered Rebecca a clear plastic bag. It contained a wallet, trapped open. The name embossed on the plastic was Dr D. W. Samuels.

But that was not what shocked Rebecca most. It was the photograph, a small, passport image of *her*. She stared at it, unable to comprehend the fact that David had carried a picture of her with him. *Her*, in his wallet. Her.

"It belongs to my husband," she said.

"When was the last time you saw him?"

"I... I can't..."

"I'm sorry to have to tell that Dr Samuels has been found dead, in Foxhill wood."

"Dead?" Her shock was genuine, shock that he really was dead, even though…just now, at the surgery….

"Fix Mrs Samuels a cup of tea will you Mayhew?" March spoke gently. "One of our dogs found him early this morning, while we were taking a last look round for that… that animal. You know about the animal?"

Rebecca nodded. "It was on the radio."

"It appears that Dr Samuels died violently." A pause. "Did you kill him Mrs Samuels?"

"No!" Rebecca cried out, then calmed herself. "He didn't come home on Friday. Our marriage…"

"Your marriage?"

"We were… are having problems."

"I'll ask you again Mrs Samuels. Did you kill your husband?"

This time Rebecca could only shake her head. The illusion that David was still alive dissolved around her. She should get them to phone the surgery… No, that would be a waste of time because her sightings of David were obviously an hallucination.

The dizziness returned. There wasn't enough oxygen in the room. She could hear March repeating her name, saw her get to her feet.

"What's going on?" Another voice and another presence.

"I'm sorry ma'am," Mayhew spluttered. "He just pushed in -"

"Alright, Sergeant, don't worry," March turned her attention to the newcomer. "And you are…?"

"I'm Dr David Samuels, and I would like to know why my house is full of police officers and my wife is so distressed."

March recovered with remarkable speed and held up the plastic bag containing the wallet. "Do you recognise this?" she asked.

David took it from her. "It's my wallet. I lost it a few days ago."

"We have your driving license as well."

"Where did you find them?"

"I think you'd better sit down Dr Samuels." March looked as if she needed to as well.

David sat beside Rebecca, and took her hand.

"We found it on a dead body and assumed the body to be… well, you."

David shrugged. "I'm alive Chief Inspector, as you can see, and no, before you ask, I don't have any brothers, a twin or otherwise."

"When did you lose your wallet and license Dr Samuels?"

"Four, five days ago. I didn't report it because I thought I'd mislaid them and that I'd find them again."

"So it looks as if they were stolen by whoever we've found in the woods."

"Yes, it does. Perhaps he was trying to steal my identity for some reason."

"Why would anyone want to do that?"

"I really have no idea."

"Are you sure?"

"Yes. He might have simply found them and was going to hand them in of course."

"How is your marriage Dr Samuels?"

"Difficult," David answered without hesitation. "The fault is mine."

"What happened on Friday?"

Friday... Oh God.

"We had a row. I walked out." David sounded genuinely ashamed.

"Your wife claims that you didn't come home."

"The row was in the morning."

"Where did you spend the night Mr Samuels?"

In a grave Inspector March.

"In my car. I drove...I wasn't thinking. I parked in a lay-by somewhere and fell asleep." David shrugged.

March paused, nodded, then said; "Alright, I think I'll leave it at that for the time being, but I may need to talk to you both again. Please don't leave the area for a few days."

Rebecca waited until the police had gone before sliding her hand free of David's. She stood, put space between them.

"Is... is my husband really dead?" she asked.

"He is. And yes, you killed him." He paused. "Look, I'm sorry I lied to you this morning, at the surgery. I was trying to reveal the truth gently. It was a mistake."

Rebecca stood, hugged herself. "He...he hurt me."

"I know he did. You were protecting yourself. He would have killed you eventually."

Rebecca turned on him. "How do you know this? Who the hell are you? What right do you have..."

Words tangled and failed.

David said. "I've been watching, for a long time."

"What do you mean watching?"

"Watching because I loved you. Ever since I first saw you I was... fascinated, bewitched. I don't know." His confusion became conviction.

"Of course I love you, he did, so must I."

A shudder tore through Rebecca. "Who are you?" she asked again.

"David Samuels," he answered.

"No, no you're not. You're some kind of stalker, or a lunatic, I don't know. Please get out of my house."

"I will if you really want me to. I'll go away and never come back. I don't mean to hurt you. I want to protect you. Haven't I done that already?"

Yes, he had.

"I'll tell you who I am, but not here. You wouldn't believe me if I told you in this room, in this house." David stood, with his hands in his trouser pockets, head bowed. "If you come with me I'll tell you who I am. If you don't, I'll leave you in peace."

He brushed past her and left the room. Rebecca heard the front door open and shut. And she was alone.

She caught up with him in the lane just as he stepped onto the verge and pushed himself into the hedge. He pulled the branches apart and waited. Beyond was a sunken path, cut through the centre of the field. There were high banks on either side where wheat merged into other, alien vegetation. As Rebecca watched, a swarm of huge insects erupted from one of the immense blooms.

She stepped onto the path, David followed. The ground was covered with a spongy green moss. The moss itself was a mass of tiny flowers.

David walked a little way then sat down on one of the banks. Rebecca joined him.

Almost immediately the giant insects swirled around them. One landed on Rebecca's knee and she was startled to see that it wasn't an insect at all, but a human-like figure; a woman with translucent wings. The woman was about four inches tall and perfectly formed. Her body, however, was covered with a fine, reddish down and her features were more feline than human. Her long, wild mane was of the same red her body hair. She opened her mouth to reveal a set of minute needle teeth then flew straight at Rebecca's face. She batted at the creature, felt an impact and heard an angry hiss as it tumbled aside.

David chuckled. Several of the creatures had landed on him and were posing suggestively.

"They are why I choose this place," David said. He loosened his tie, undid his top button and folded his shirt sleeves a few times. "To help you believe."

"What are they?" Rebecca no longer fought to suspend disbelief.

"You'd call them fairies. We call them Sajanath. They're not very bright and they don't grant wishes…well, not magical ones."

"We?"

David turned his face to the sun, closed his eyes and said. "I am the real David Samuels. The David Samuels you killed was an impostor."

Rebecca did not respond.

David sighed. "All right, here we go. Are you ready for this?"

"Just tell me."

"Ok, according to folklore, if you leave a newborn baby outside, the fairy folk will steal it and leave a Changeling in its place." Another pause. "It's true. Sometimes the…the fairy folk as you call them, do steal human babies, and replace them with inferior versions. Not very often, however, because the replacements are hard to make and often die."

"Why do they steal babies?" Rebecca decided to go along with this and see where it led.

"Because the… Look they're not fairy folk, they're P, I'll explain in a moment. It's disastrous for the People to mate with each other, I suppose their gene pool is worn up, I don't know, but if they breed with humans. . ."

"So what you're telling me is that the David Samuels I married was a, what did call it?"

"A Changeling."

Rebecca sighed, and felt an overwhelming desire to laugh. Here she was, in a fantasyland in the middle of a Suffolk wheat field, plagued by fairies and discovering that she had been married to an artificial man created out of some magical vat. The laughter died away. The artificial man had been human and she had taken his life.

"Who are the P?" she asked.

"They've been called a lot of things; devils and angels, giants, men of renown."

"Which are you?"

David smiled, there was a familiar mischief in that smile. "Human."

"What do you want from me?"

"I want to love you."

Though strangely moved by his answer, by those words falling from *those* lips, Rebecca shook her head. "I can't. You're not…"

"I want to protect you. I can save you from the trouble, you're in."

Rebecca surged to her feet, disturbing a swarm of Sajanath in the process. They angered her, all of it angered her. "You're not David," she said with a firmness that startled her. "You're a complete stranger."

"Am I?"

She spun round, something in his tone. "What do you mean by that?"

"There were times…when Dr Samuels was out on call, when I…"

God… Oh God… Rebecca backed away. "You… you bastard!" she snarled, startled by the expletive, yet feeling something released with its utterance. She spun round and stumbling blindly along the cut. Sajanath swarmed at her approach, one darted at her and was rewarded with a blow. David called after her, she didn't care. She had to get away from him. It was rape wasn't it? A violation. Oh God, every fucking man she met wanted to hurt her in some way.

Fucking, yes that was a good word, a fine, liberating collection of sounds that she wanted to scream in his face. She reached the hedge. A car swished by on the other side. A lark sang high overhead. She pushed at the branches, flinched to protect her eyes. She pushed and probed, and suddenly found the gap, so obvious, yet so hidden. She stumbled out onto the road. There was her cottage, her car, and the BMW with its boot full of evidence.

Indoors was the shower that became a flesh-scourging exorcism in a steam filled cell. She leaned against the wall in the scalding rain, head down, sobbing. The world was full of lies. Her life…Everything was slipping from her grasp. She let go, slid to the floor, huddled against one glass wall.

And remembered.

Those times. In the quiet darkness, when it seemed that everything was alright. When it seemed that it was worthwhile. When there was no violence, no despair. It had been a rape, yet…yet it had given her peace. Bayfield's violation was violent and foul. The David thing's violation had been sweet and gentle. It had been a gift to her.

She lifted her face and let the water tear at her skin.

A movement caught her attention, something in the steam-mist. A figure, indistinct, as if only partly formed, and waiting.

Rebecca sensed that a decision was required of her.

He was offering her a chance wasn't he? Was offering a love she had already tasted, unknowingly, and found to be good. He was offering her protection, new worlds, wonders, perhaps even some chance of redemption. Why not try? She had fractured her own world beyond repair, why not step out of it?

Now.

She hugged herself, still afraid of the shadow.

Then whispered; "Yes."

Chapter Seven

Three-am silence enfolded itself around her as she sat at the desk in a room she visited rarely, and not at all since she had killed its owner. David's study was a sparse, tidy place that boasted a filing cabinet, the desk at which she now sat, a computer and a small bookshelf lined with medical volumes and journals. It was small, closed-in, private and so redolent of Dr Samuels, so shaped like him, so moulded about him, that, even now, she felt like a trespasser.

The other David, the allegedly *Real* David, was asleep. Until a few minutes ago his right arm had been wrapped around her, warm flutters of his breath had shivered over the back of her neck. His semen was sticky on the inside of her thighs and tainted the clinical austerity of the study with its faint, slippery-sweet bouquet. The acceptance, which glowed deep in her, of this bizarre, sick reality, this supernatural joke, was more terrifying than the joke itself and despite a post-coital contentment she could not deny, had kept her wide awake.

It was while on her way to the bathroom that she noticed the study door. It had always been there, of course, but this time she *noticed* it. Her breath caught, her heart accelerated into a ragged hammering. She wanted to go in. She *had* to go in, driven by the same desire that had made her push her fingers into the fresh-turned soil of David's grave.

She jabbed at the door, jerking back as it swung open as if the wood was red hot. Nothing happened. She went inside, flicked on the light and was surprised to see a Bible open on the desk. As far as she was aware, David had not left the bed since they had made love (was that what it was? Could you make *love* with a stranger?). So unless Dr Samuels had really returned from the grave (no longer so impossible in a world that now included demons and goblins) he had been reading the Bible and had left it here, open, never to return to finish whatever passage he was studying for…what? Instruction? Comfort?

Even more shattering was the fact that the Bible was hers, a Sunday School reward for "good attendance and diligent study."

There was something touching about the sight of that Bible. Like the photograph in David's wallet, another connection between Rebecca and the man she had killed. Another proof that he loved her.

There's only one Rebecca. . .

The passage was from the Song of Solomon, book that Pastor Emerson of the Brilliant Smile had seldom preached from. When he did, it was always as a metaphor for Christ and His p, which made no sense to Rebecca because the language seemed so obviously sensual.

Outside, something moaned, the sound an anguished howl of rage that rose into an animal bellow. Rebecca's breath caught in her throat. The house was under siege again. She returned her attention to the computer.

There was another moan, a snarl.

Rebecca hurried back to the bedroom, where the darkness was stained blue by the perpetual, ice-flamed candle. It was the source of what David called the *Circle*, the protective barrier that had burned the creature in the garden.

The curtain billowed in the night breeze. Rebecca went to the window.

"It's alright," David said sleepily. "They can't come in."

Rebecca shut the window anyway then climbed into the bed beside David. The action was natural, disturbingly ordinary. She settled into his arms. To hell with it. To hell with the insanity of what he said and did, to hell with guilt and shame. Dr Samuels had beaten her and knocked her down and one night she had fought back. Now she was safe. She deserved this.

Didn't she?

Didn't she?

Rebecca pushed herself deeper into David's arms. This was safety. This was where she must stay. Her mouth searched for, and found, his. Her breath was warm, his hot.

No more questions. No more thought.

He had to go in the morning of course, to maintain the fiction of Dr Samuels. Rebecca asked him how he could ply the profession without being trained. He simply looked at her and smiled, and she remembered Mrs Etheridge's tears of joy and understood. Then he was gone and the house was empty and all manner of fear came back.

Rebecca forced herself into activity because David's mother was coming that afternoon.

It didn't stop the house being empty.

Or screaming *guilty* at her. It *accused*; every piece of furniture, every landmark, each one a Station of the Cross. This is the chair he was sitting in when she had arrived home late from Lynne's...this is where he brushed past her on his way to the garage...

* * *

They arrived before David came home. It started with Dr Jonathon Samuels' friendly shout of "Anyone in?" from the open conservatory door. Jonathon was a kindly, amiable man who usually let his wife do most of the talking.

"Come in," Rebecca exuded false warmth and covered her panic in a tight, welcoming hug. When it was done, Jonathan held her at arms length and frowned. "You're looking pale my dear. Are you sure it's alright for us to stay?"

"Of course it is," Rebecca lied. "It's so nice to see you."

"Mary's in the garden at the moment," Jonathon said. "Her usual tour of inspection. Those flowers had better come to attention or she'll want to know why."

Mary always walked round the garden before coming in, unless it was raining or exceptionally cold. Rebecca could see her now through the kitchen window, a short, stocky woman with ruthlessly permed white hair. There was something Churchillian about her stance, obvious even from this distance.

"Coffee?" Rebecca offered.

Jonathan grinned his wide, face-crumpling grin and said "Absolutely. That drive up here seems to get longer every time we make it."

"We'll come to see *you* next time." We? Who was *We* exactly? And that was when the guilt came back, a thunderous tempest that burned the truth bright into her mind. I killed your son. I killed him, three days ago. They've even found his body and they'll probably want to talk to you eventually. . .

He hurt me, he beat me, and now he's dead.

Jonathan was speaking. ". . .is lovely. You keep it well Rebecca." A mischievous wink. "I know you do most of the gardening. That son of mine never was one for getting soil on his hands. But car grease, now that's a different matter. That Humber still your biggest rival for his affections?"

"Yes." She surprised herself with a passable imitation of a laugh. Oh and I used one of his tools to kill him, then the hoist to load him into the boot of the BMW. She bustled round the kitchen, losing herself in a grey numbness of action. She filled the kettle, switched it on, unhooked mugs, hunted down the coffee jar and retrieved milk from the refrigerator.

Jonathan was talking happily; the journey again, the traffic, the weather, too hot for his liking, although, oddly, he didn't mind the heat when they holidayed abroad. Different kind of heat he supposed. On and on, his amiable chatter, easy conversation, not needing a response, only some semblance of an audience.

By the time Rebecca had filled one mug with coffee and two with tea, Mary had worked her way indoors. There was a brief hug and kiss, more formal than the one between Jonathan and Rebecca. Mary had not forgiven her for marrying her son, although she had softened a great deal since the early days.

Another comment on her complexion followed the cursory hug, another lie about tiredness and headaches. Then it was into the sitting room, where Mary placed herself firmly, and decisively in the armchair by the fireplace and Rebecca held herself together by a combination of willpower and fear. Suddenly she wanted to blurt out the truth. "But it's alright," she would finish. "Because I have a replacement son for you. Actually he claims to be your real son and I think believe him."

Instead the conversation toured the garden, and included a grudging acknowledgement that Rebecca was keeping it beautiful. Mary too had found the journey tiring; too much traffic, everyone driving too fast. Jonathan, sitting beside Rebecca on the sofa, sipped coffee and uttered sporadic support to his wife's monologue.

The kitchen called. Rebecca offered her apologies, promised that David would be home any moment and fled.

As she stirred gravy she saw David standing in the middle of the lawn. He wore his white shirt and silver-blue tie. His hands were in his pockets and he was staring at the house. As was the way with this new David, his top button was loosened and his sleeves part-rolled.

Rebecca removed a saucepan from the heat and went out to him. She stumbled to a halt a few feet away. He looked at her, stricken, in the way Dr Samuels would look stricken when Rebecca was sprawled on the floor, head spinning from a blow, nose bleeding and waiting for shock to become pain.

"They're here," he said at last.

"Yes," Rebecca answered carefully.

David nodded, bit his lip, and frowned. "In the house?"

Where else? Rebecca nodded.

"Are they okay?"

"Are you?"

He looked at her, as if for the first time. It was his turn to nod. Then he shook his head. "I'm not okay Rebecca. She's my mother. He's my father. And I don't remember them."

"I could tell them you've had to stay on at work -"

"No. I need to see them." Without a further word, he strode towards the house.

Rebecca arrived in the sitting room about ten seconds after David. He stood in front of the armchair as his mother got to her feet. Her determined struggle was *not* to be assisted.

She stood still for a moment and looked hard at her son. When she uttered his name she sounded as if she was struggling against tears. And when Rebecca stepped round behind the sofa she saw that tears actually were streaming down her face.

"David?" Mary repeated, voice tremulous and weak. She gasped, and then she was in David's arms. Worried, Jonathan leaned forward to ask if she was alright.

Mary broke away, flustered, fumbling for a tissue. "Good gracious," she blustered. "What on earth came over me?" She laughed, an unusual reaction for Mary Samuels. "Getting sentimental in my old age."

She looked round the room, her cheeks red, her eyes shining. Then she sat down again and stared once more at her son as he turned to shake hands with his father. Jonathan was on his feet. "Hello David," he said. Then he too seemed to falter. The handshake became a prolonged clasp and a silent exchange of some emotion, some realisation that the older man did not appear to understand.

Later that night, when the house was silent and the moon at its brightest, Rebecca woke to find David gone from her bed. Her search for him ended in the conservatory. The patio door was open. She hesitated on the threshold. It was not good to go outside at night, there were things out there, things that moaned and stalked the house. But tonight the garden was quiet. She saw David, walking slowly along the left hand border. He was naked. Half-silvered, by the moon, half shadowed.

"Can't sleep?" she asked him.

"Mustn't sleep," he answered. "I have to push the Circle further out while my parents are here. I don't want them, to hear…" It was then that Rebecca noticed the flame, flickering in his open palm.

"What are they?" she asked. "Those things, out there."

David stopped walking, and sat down, cross-legged on the grass. Rebecca sat beside him. The ground was damp but she didn't care.

"I shouldn't be here," David said. "I've broken laws. They want me back."

Rebecca shivered, glanced about herself involuntarily.

David slid an arm about her shoulders. "Some of them are too bestial to understand. The attack must have been terrifying for you."

"Everything is terrifying. Every breath I take scares me."

"Perhaps I should leave you be. You're safe from the police now -"

"No!" She would go insane if he went away. She could not be alone anymore.

He shushed her gently, held her close and nuzzled her hair. "*I* should have killed him," he said. "I saw what he did to you, I should have taken him away and taken his place and you would never have known."

"*I* would have."

A pause, then. "She's dying," David said. "My mother. She's going to die of a stroke, soon. I can feel her death moving through her body."

"Couldn't you heal her, the way you healed Elizabeth Etheridge?"

"It's different for my mother. It's her time. We all have our time. To interfere is…wrong."

"I'm sorry," Rebecca said and thought her words feeble.

"I want to go home with them. I need to spend some time with her, before it's too late."

Another panic. "Can't it wait a few days? Until I get used to…until things settle down." She couldn't be alone. Not so soon after finding him. "And the police want us to stay here."

"I don't have a few days. Her time is too close. I want to be there when it happens. I'll come to you if the police return."

Rebecca knew she couldn't be selfish. She deserved nothing anyway. "Of course you must go," she said quietly. "Do you want me to come with you?"

"No, not this time. The Circle will keep you safe. I'll only be gone two, three days at the most."

Mary Samuel's life, measured now in days.

Third Intermezzo

Nine years ago. . .

When, after the fire, there had indeed been a still, small voice.

It came from inside and it would not stop.

"This is your fault," it murmured in venomous accents that were hers-but-not-hers.

Yes it was her fault. She should have ignored Dr David Samuels' words, no matter how harsh. She should have allowed him to rant the poisons out of himself. But she hadn't. She, Rebecca Ann Samuels, had taken it personally and when her defence crumbled, resorted to a defiant and emotionally suicidal attack.

And now she lay on the bed, in the dark, her face aflame. A bruise would emerge from the nest of shattered veins that webbed her right cheek in a day or so. The bruises on her heart and soul were already fully formed.

Something had changed that night, the universe wrenched out of kilter so hard and so far that, surely, it could never recover its original form.

Rebecca had sensed that things were wrong the way an animal sniffs out the onset of natural cataclysm. Little things came first, tiny irritations and minor impatience, all expressed through a forced smile. "You know I don't like minced beef," he had said, one evening, what was it, a week ago? Difficult to judge when your husband's duties were not entirely nine-to-five and there were no children to force you into school day time-structures.

Rebecca had been out to lunch with some friends – well, other women her age - from the village. Many of them were the same women who had shunned her during their teenage years. Being a GP's wife obviously brought her the kudos necessary for acceptance into their white-toothed, sharp-taloned circle.

The lunch was leisurely, with a ten mile trip to the nearest supermarket to follow. Panic set in. Rebecca was late and tired, she grabbed the quickest, easiest ingredients from the shelves; spaghetti, pasta sauce, tinned mushrooms and, God forbid, minced beef.

David's smiled "You know I don't like minced beef," was redolent of last straws and terminal exasperation. She apologised, reached out to hold his hand and tell him that she wouldn't make the mistake again and that she had been so stupid and –

He jerked his hand away and snapped, "It doesn't matter." Which meant, of course, it mattered one hell of a lot.

More and more things "didn't matter". The smile became more fixed, the eyes harder, and sadder. Stress, Rebecca decided and set about trying to make life at home easier for him. The harder she tried, however, the more mistakes she made

She had asked him the question yesterday.

Dr Samuels sat in the armchair working through some paperwork. Radio Three whispered Vaughn March' 3rd Symphony. Rebecca stood at the window, hugging a thick, full-length cardigan about herself as she watched the late autumn afternoon bloody the lower sky.

No answer from the armchair, only the rustle of paperwork and a sigh of weariness.

Rebecca asked again. "What's wrong David?"

"What the hell are you talking about?"

"You've been…I don't know. A bit irritable I suppose." No he hadn't. That was one thing he hadn't been. He had been attentive in many ways, needing her close, stroking her hair as she sat on the floor, curled against his knees, holding her tight as they lay together in the dark.

"I've been irritable?" He sounded genuinely surprised. "Are you joking Rebecca?"

"No -"

"I was wondering what was wrong with you."

Rebecca turned to look at him, unable to believe what she had just heard. "What have I done?" Apart from the minced beef.

"I don't know." Impatiently, accompanied by a shrug and attention returned to whatever form he was filling in. "Just leave me alone, okay?"

Suddenly the paperwork was swept to the floor and Rebecca was following her husband through the kitchen, the connecting door and into the garage. She knew she shouldn't, that she was acting like a kicked puppy looking for forgiveness. But she couldn't endure this fracture in their relationship. She wanted to repair it somehow, any how.

"Fuck off," David barked, white-shirted and cuff-linked among the grease and oil.

"What did you say? David, what did you just say to me?"

"You heard."

"No, no you don't talk to me like that." Hurt made her brave. "Don't you ever tell me to…you know. Please don't."

"I'm tired, okay? I've had a shitty day."

"I didn't mean to…" God, how she hated that stung, whiney voice of hers. "I'm sorry David."

"Always bloody sorry. Why are you so fucking useless that you have to live one long apology?"

And more, delivered in a spray of spittle, all red face and fire-hot eyes.

She screamed back. And saw herself, as red-faced and rage-distorted as her husband, hair wild, tears streaming down her face, nose running, arms waving, screaming.

Then she was stumbling backwards, vision blurred, face on fire, spiralling away from David until a bare-brick wall slammed into her back and there was no more storm, just a white silence that filled every part of her mind and flesh. A brutal pulse drove into her teeth and up into her left eye.

And there was David, soft-focussed through a curtain of hair, huddled into himself like a frightened child, fists still clenched, arm across his chest in a frozen follow-through.

Rebecca went to bed, where she lay in the dark with that still, small voice.

Nine years later she had lost count of how many blows, fresh starts and healings had taken place. On and on it went.

Until the night she picked up a hammer with an oil-darkened handle and pterodactyl head. . .

Chapter Eight

Rebecca watched Jonathon Samuels' car crunch off the gravel and out onto the lane and it was terrible. David was in the front beside his father, Mary was in the rear. They waved and Rebecca waved back. She added a smile, a humourless stretch of lips over teeth.

The engine sound took a long time to fade and as she stood in the entrance to her drive, Rebecca tried to comprehend the fact that that was the last time she would see Mary Samuels alive. How *did* you comprehend such a thing? You didn't. The same way you didn't comprehend the fact that you had killed someone. Some emergency system tripped in and rammed the confusion, fear and debilitating grief into a dark cerebral corner then turned you away from the empty road and hurried you into the back garden to clear away the remains of the final al fresco dinner she had served.

There was a sudden chill in the air as the sun disappeared behind the hedge.

It would start soon. She sensed that she was already being watched. Not from here, but from somewhere distant. She hurried indoors.

A return trip. The light had changed again. She moved quickly to clear the remaining debris of the meal. Three steps from the conservatory she heard a sliding sound, the crack of twigs, something big, just on the far side of the hedge. Memories of the creatures she had encountered in Foxhill Woods bubbled to the surface.

Indoors, she crashed the tray onto a worktop then rushed around the house to check doors and windows and close curtains despite the remaining vestiges of daylight. She switched on the television. A soap opera was playing. It would do.

And was she beautiful?

She blinked. What?

Well, was she beautiful?

She had never considered it before. Dr Samuels (she thought of him as that now, David was someone new) had told her she was beautiful. He had repeated it over and over, as if unable to comprehend that someone like him should be given such a boon from the Gods of Love. Dr Samuels, of the square jaw and dark hair, the hope of every single female in Abbotsfield. Dr Samuels, who had slapped them all in the face by marrying that dowdy weirdo Rebecca Wright. Rebecca understood his lack of self-esteem now. He had known that he was an impostor, a second rate copy. Somewhere, deep down in what constituted a Changeling's sub-conscious the knowledge of his inferiority, of his falseness, had festered and boiled and, when it could be contained no longer, hurled solar flares of rage surface-wards.

He hit her.

He kept her photograph in his wallet.

He read her Bible.

But that wasn't the point. The point was whether or not she was beautiful.

Rebecca reared to her feet and ran upstairs to the bedroom, where she yanked open the wardrobe door. There she was, that pale, gauche woman in a sleeveless yellow summer dress. She didn't exactly fill it well did she? And her hair, mediocre mouse-brown, not blonde, not red, just brown. What about her face? Too long, too thin, her eyes, watery and sad and frightened. If there was any beauty, she couldn't see it.

David said it was there. So it didn't matter.

Yes it did.

She was a fool to think she was anything. She snarled at her reflection. Fool! Stupid bitch! She ground out the words in silence. Her eyes blazed. Look at you, you miserable, wretched murdering bitch. Who the fuck do you think you are?

She grabbed at her hair and yanked at it. She was nothing. She was dirt, she was bones and flesh and murderer and blood and nothing else. Look at her, look, look look! She slammed her fists onto the mirror. The glass cracked with a loud snap. The sound startled her and the mouse-haired little bitch with the miserable figure and frightened eyes retreated into her sliced and distorted universe. There was a shard of glass on the carpet. She picked it up and saw part of her own left eye, borne down by a frown. She lifted the glass and slashed it across her cheek.

Outside, things screeched and howled

Rebecca reached up and felt blood, warm and free flowing. Sobbing she ran into the bathroom.

There was another mirror in there. She forced herself to look. The cut wasn't deep, thank God, but it was bleeding messily.

Was she beautiful? Was she, was she WAS SHE? She lifted her fists again, then stopped herself. She couldn't break every mirror in the house. But she couldn't bear her reflection either. Couldn't bear looking at that filthy, murdering, ugly, cow.

The light. She spun round and fumbled for the pull switch. It bounced and flicked out of her grasp. She caught it, tugged, and reduced her reflection to shadowed, vagueness.

Struggling for breath she rushed through the house, extinguishing lights and closing curtains. Even the television had to be turned off. She stood in the middle of the kitchen. The dark enfolded and hid her. From outside came the bestial rage of her besiegers.

She switched on the radio and evening jazz played.

Wait.

She had forgotten the bedroom light.

Back upstairs she hesitated in front of the bedroom door. She must have slammed it shut when she fled the room. Rebecca opened it carefully, not wanting to catch a glimpse of herself in the broken mirror. She reached into the room without looking, searched for, then found, the switch. Click. Darkness…No, there was a cold blue glow, uncertain, shifting.

Steeling herself, Rebecca went inside. She crossed to the candle, licked her fingertips and crushed the sapphire flame. Ice stung her flesh. The flame flared. It should have died instantly, but it flared and spilled blindingly.

Then died.

And Rebecca knew she was beautiful enough and that her reflection was harmless -

Oh God…The candle…The Circle…

Appalled she slumped onto the bed and tried to remember why she had been so utterly stupid, suicidal in fact. Because something out there had made her do it.

There was a loud animal howl from outside. It sounded like triumph. Matches. She needed matches. Would ordinary matches work? She had to try. Dear Jesus. Something had tricked her into this and she had fallen for it and now she was going to die. She lurched through the dark to the bedroom door and was almost through before she realised that she could switch on the electric light.

She ran downstairs, almost tripping, clinging to the rail. Something thudded against the landing window. Something else clattered over the roof. She made it to the bottom and without hesitation, switched on the next light and raced along the passage towards the kitchen.

Through the door.

Kitchen light.

Across to the drawer where the odds and ends were kept.

She scrabbled through the contents; fuses, elastic bands, light bulbs, packs of drawing pins…matches! Thank you God, matches.

A loud thud. Then a crack.

Glass-crack.

She looked up. The kitchen window blind was down. Beyond it, something pummelled the glass. Another crack, the report, gun-shot sharp. Rebecca jumped back, uttered an involuntary cry. A moment later glass erupted into the sink, over the work top and onto the kitchen floor. A bruise-coloured, ludicrously long arm flickered in. A taloned claw groped for purchase and found the front edge of the sink. Stringy muscles tensed and its owner crashed through the blinds.

This time there was a knife in Rebecca's hand, a wide-bladed Laserknife from the rack on the wall behind her. She didn't remember snatching it up, but that didn't matter. It was knife and she was terrified and cornered and possessed of an animal terror that erupted out of her as rage.

That rage, the one that had clawed blood from Jim Bayfield's hand and wielded a hammer against Dr Samuels.

One of the spider-limbed apes was in the kitchen, its legs and arms outspread over the worktops, its tiny body suspended between them, its small-eyed, vast mouthed head open in a snarl of hungry triumph.

A swipe of its claw was met with a desperate slash from Rebecca. Her blade bounced from bony, sinewy flesh. There was a gout of foul smelling white liquid and a deafening cacophony of shrieks.

Rebecca stumbled to the left, unbalanced by the wild blow. The creature recoiled, waving its injured limb like a whip, spraying rancid life-fluid and smashing the stacked crockery from the evening meal onto the floor.

Another came through, shoved its injured comrade aside and leapt at Rebecca, arms akimbo, jaws wide. Instinct again, a mindless force that made her ram the knife forward, its handle gripped in two hands. There was an impact that sent her back against the wall, which she hit with a grunt of expelled air. The creature's tiny body slammed into her, its huge head snapped forward and cracked against her left shoulder and for a moment, an instant, a heartbeat, its icy, dead-fowl cheek was resting against hers. Then it dropped to the floor and shivered as if cold. The knife handle projected from its sunken belly.

Rebecca spun round and fled the kitchen. She made the front door but something was pounding the double-glazing. From the kitchen came sounds of more of the ape-things.

She thundered upstairs, slipped, cracked her knee, and drove herself on until she was in the bedroom, door bolted behind her. She glanced round; the dressing table, better than nothing.

A weight hit the bedroom door, claws scrabbled at the wood.

Crying with effort, Rebecca hauled the dressing table across the room and shoved it against the door as tightly as she was able. Exhausted she rested against it for a few seconds then hurried back to the candle. She pulled the matches from her pocket. Shaking hands spilled matches until she managed to grasp one and strike it against the side of the box.

There was a scuttling across the roof, wings beat at the bedroom window, and something hissed. As the front door exploded inwards and a roar filled the house, loud enough to rattle the windows, Rebecca applied the fragile flame to the candle. The wick shrivelled and crumbled and did not catch. No…Oh God no…

From outside the howls and screeches reached apocalyptic proportions. Rebecca straightened and stared at the bedroom door which now trembled in its frame. The dressing table was flung onto its side as the door crashed open.

Chapter Nine

And in it came. This one huge. It kicked the dressing table aside and loomed over Rebecca. She felt her strength drain, felt herself spiral into a mind-roar of terror.

Yet there was also acceptance.

That other, accepting, part of her was a cool observer. As her knees failed, and she sank floorwards, it puzzled over the bizarre structure of her nemesis. The creature's solid, stocky torso was set atop a pair of muscular legs, but it only had one arm. A knotted, vast limb that concluded with a huge, three fingered hand. What grew from the other shoulder was not an arm at all, but a neck, wormlike, ending in what was little more than a swelling filled entirely by two large, curious eyes.

Now on her hands and knees, Rebecca wondered if she should lower her head so she wouldn't see the blow coming.

The creature spoke. Its mouth was in its abdomen, a wide toothless splitting of flesh. "Lady," it said. Its voice was deep and gruff and heavily accented. "Lady, are yuh well?"

She nodded, which was insane, because she was far from well and waiting to be slaughtered.

"Who… Who are you?" she managed at last.

"Bezzec," the creature answered. "Can I get yuh anyfing?"

Get her… she tried to see beyond him to the horde of spider apes who had pursued her through the house. There was no sign or sound of them. Did that mean that they were gone, or dead, or simply waiting for this their leader to perform the coup de grace?

Then it moved, lifted its arm, opened its fist.

Rebecca moaned and shrank away.

A cold blue flame coiled and flickered in Bezzec's open palm. "Suckle," he said. As he moved carefully past her, towards the candle she had extinguished, Rebecca realised that he had meant "Circle."

"Did David send for you?" Rebecca hardly dared ask the question.

"Ah," It sounded like an affirmative.

Rebecca waved towards the shattered bedroom door. "Where are the…"

"Cuthella brucked."

Brucked? Broked? Broken?

Blue-white flared, Bezzec's head swung round to stare at Rebbeca. "Are yuh well?" he repeated. The separation of eyes and mouth gave the disconcerting impression of two beings in one body. For all Rebecca knew, that might be the case.

"Thank you, yes." She struggled to her feet. Her legs were still weak and she was dizzy. She glanced toward the landing, and saw an outflung, overlong limb. Definitely 'brucked'. "Are you alone?" Rebecca asked.

"Ah." His body now swung way from the candle. Bezzec was naked, seemed male enough, yet was completely devoid of any obvious genitalia. "I suv the Libby Raider."

"Libby…" Rebecca sat down on the bed, unable to remain on her feet any longer.

"Davud, the Libby Raider."

"I see." She didn't, but suddenly she was shaking, too exhausted for questions and explanations. Her teeth chattered, her muscles and joints ached. She lay down, while, without a further word, Bezzec lumbered out onto the landing. It was a while before she heard him descend the stairs and assumed that he had cleared up. The image of him heading for the wrecked front door, burdened with a tangle of broken spider apes - Cuthella he had called them – was too vivid for comfort. After a few more seconds, there was silence again. Rebecca rolled over and stared at the blue flame.

So why wasn't she a screaming, gibbering wreck? Could it be that she was getting used to this insanity? And just who was David, the Libby Raider? What position did he hold in that weird society in which he lived that he could summon up a helper like Bezzec? Or perhaps Bezzec was a professional security guard, or a mercenary of some sort.

Then the shock finally hit her.

And she lay, holding herself tight as she sobbed and shook, afraid and so, utterly guilty.

She awoke, sitting upright against the sofa. Her head resounded to the crashing skull-thunder of a hangover. Vague recollections floated in the grey murk of pain; a stumble downstairs and into the lounge, a fumble through the drink cabinet and a swig from the first bottle that fell into her trembling hand. It was scotch, liquid fire that scorched its way into her stomach. She had done this before, when bruised and reeling with shock and humiliation.

There was a damp patch beside her and on her nightshirt. The damp issued alcohol fumes so intense that they made her want to be sick. Not moving her head, she felt for the bottle, and turned it upright.

It was daylight, late morning according to the clock.

She went to bed.

After a day spent slipping in and out of consciousness Rebecca was finally awakened by someone shouting her name.

Rebecca's forced open her eyes. The light, though changed, was still painful.

She pulled on a dressing gown and shouted back that she was coming. The shouting went on, closer now, someone halfway up the stairs by the sound of it. Rebecca steadied herself then went out onto the landing. Light speared in from the smashed front door and seared Rebecca's optic nerves all the way to her disintegrating brain. There was a figure, silhouetted and indistinct. Rebecca didn't recognise the visitor until a voice demanded to know what the hell had happened here.

"Nothing...a fight..." Rebecca and pushed hair off her face and watched Lynne step out of the gold-yellow inferno.

"My God Rebecca."

"Just a hangover, don't worry."

"But this place...You said a fight. What sort of fight?"

"Monsters," Rebecca answered without thinking. It was the truth, and she had no other explanation handy.

"Is he here?"

"What?" Focussing through the pain was difficult.

"Is David here?"

"No... He's gone to stay with his parents. His mother..."

"Jesus Rebecca, who gives a fuck about his mother?"

"She's dying –"

Lynne shook her head, her face ashen. "Thank God he did this to the house and not you."

"He didn't –" Rebecca stopped herself. It was no use trying to explain.

"I'm so bloody disappointed in you. I thought you'd found a little courage at last, but no, he's back, trampling all over you again. I mean, look at this...this...God it's like a battlefield." Lynne broke off abruptly and turned away. Then she seemed to come to a decision. "I'm going to the police."

"No. Lynne no –"

She was already at the ruined front door before Rebecca managed to set off in pursuit. Lynne disappeared into the blaze of yellow sun-fire she had emerged from and by the time Rebecca rushed outside, she was gone. Rebecca called her name, and was answered by the thump of a car door. The engine started moments before Rebecca reached the entrance to the drive. When she stumbled out into the road, all she saw were the tail lights of Lynne's Mini, bright in the gathering murk as it raced out of sight.

For a moment Rebecca wanted to jump into her own car and follow. Lynne was a good friend. She would be an invaluable ally. The other thing could be sorted out -

Rebecca froze.

She was outside. Not only that, she was outside the Circle. She looked round, scanned the road, the hedgerows. She listened, tried to catch the sounds that had become part of the night.

The silence terrified her.

She backed carefully towards the cottage. She felt gravel under her feet and swung round, ready to sprint the remaining distance to the front door.

And cried out as a figure detached itself from the lengthening shadows.

Bezzec.

"Gorn," he snarled. "All gorn." His head snaked out, twisted this way and that. "Searus buznuss."

"Are you sure?" Rebecca asked him.

"Ah."

"But why would they..." A thought slithered in. Would she, Rebecca, still be a threat if whatever David belonged to had taken him back? Had he created a Circle at his parent's house? How many of those candles did he have?

She rushed indoors, snatched up the telephone and fumbled the number for Jonathon and Mary Samuels. No answer, ten rings and an ansafone. Okay, perhaps they were out, or Mary had been taken ill. She tried Mary's mobile. It was off. Father-in-law's asked for a message. Rebecca hung up, steadied herself then rang Mary's local hospitals, Watford first, then Hemel Hempstead. There was an agony of connections, a check of records.

Mary Samuels was not in either hospital. No one was answering their phones. The monsters had gone...

Rebecca grabbed the car key and was actually at the front door before she realised that she was still wearing her dressing gown.

Chapter Ten

Rebecca Ann Samuels' second desperate journey also began with a maddened, headlong dash along narrow lanes. This one, however, was accomplished in her hatchback rather than the BMW, and took her out of the countryside and onto the A12. And his time her passenger was alive and folded awkwardly into the front seat instead of into the boot. Bezzec had insisted that he came with her because he had prummussed the Libby Raider that he would protect Rebecca and prumusses should not be braked.

The A12 was surprisingly busy. The endless procession of yellow-white headlamps lanced into Rebecca's eyes and poked her all-but dormant hangover back to life.

It wasn't until she was racing over the graceful curve of the Orwell Bridge that she felt afraid. Before there had been a panic that had no link with actual fear, an adrenalin-fuelled rush that forced her to dress in the same jeans and tee shirt she had worn for her Sunday morning stroll in the woods and throw the thick zip-up cardigan and also a heavy coat onto the back seat.

Now, as Radio Two played Herbie Hancock's "Cantaloupe Island", the reality slammed into Rebecca and suddenly she was glad of the brooding, nightmare presence that was Bezzec.

Perhaps this was a fool's errand. Perhaps David and his parents were sitting quietly on the patio at their home, sipping wine and looking up at the stars, or, worse, though still sane, gathered about Mary's deathbed. And Rebecca was about to blunder in, hot, bothered and panting apologies before being told to sit down and have a glass of wine. Or even a nice cup of tea.

Could you make that two cups? I have friend in the car…

But Bezzec had said that it was serious.

Herbie Hancock yielded to Art Blakey, who's Jazz Messengers delivered the jaunty "Are You Real?" Now there was a question.

"What is a Libby Raider?"

Bezzec's worm-like neck coiled round from his far shoulder to bring his spherical head close to Rebecca. She tried not to flinch back. "Nut Libby Raider. Li-bby-rai-der. He'll save us from The Wuman."

"Liberator? Is that it? David is the Liberator?"

"Ah."

Next question, just waiting to be asked.

"She rules," was Bezzec's answer.

"Rules what? Is she one of the People?"

"She rules our corner of the Place."

"So, what are you Bezzec?" The question sounded rude, but polite social shadow-boxing didn't seem appropriate at the moment.

"Cast-Out."

"Cast... Cast-Out?"

"The ugly and the unwanted."

"David's going to lead a revolt against this Woman, is that it?"

"Ah."

And it's all occurring in those unnoticed lanes and pathways that existed right under the noses of the good people of Abbotsfield and beyond.

They reached the slip road onto the M25 at nine-fifteen in the evening. Rebecca took her car up onto the north section, heading west. There were signs to Watford and Heathrow.

The petrol was low. Rebecca didn't want to stop. There was no time for delays. Running out of petrol, however, would mean the biggest delay of all.

Two tunnels then a relentlessly monotonous stretch of motorway brought them to the South Mimms service area. There was a roundabout, a set of tricky lane changes followed by the bright blaze of shops, and fast food outlets that ignited a coffee craving. Rebecca pulled into the petrol station, cut the engine and climbed out of the car.

She glanced around the forecourt. There were several vehicles, p, but no one seemed interested in her hatchback, or its immense passenger. There was shadow enough to darken the interiors of the waiting cars and vans, despite the stark lighting

Rebecca shivered as she worked the pump. The night was chilly and –

Not empty.

She spun round to see –

An overweight, overall-clad van driver share an obscene joke with his passengers, a woman clipped towards the shop.

A child cried.

No... not a child. The cry was...wrong somehow. The van driver started and looked round.

Again.

Rebecca's vitals turned liquid. She had heard that cry many times outside her own house. It was the song of the Cuthella.

Movement, something skirted the edge of the petrol station.

The petrol pump indicator counted the litres.

The van driver made for the shop, in a hurry now, no more jokes. The clipping woman returned to her sports car.

There... A shape, bounding along the edges of the forecourt light-island.

"Fuck!" shouted the van driver and scrambled through the door into the shop.

The woman stopped halfway to her sports car and peered into the dark beyond the pumps.

A third car swept onto the forecourt, momentarily obscuring the figure. When it slid to halt beside a vacant pump, the creature was gone.

Rebecca wrenched the pump nozzle from her car. The tank was half full. It would suffice. Her presence had made this place dangerous. There was a family in that new car; children, an elderly lady.

Rebecca set off towards the shop and met the van driver, ashen-faced, running back to his vehicle. Rebecca heard the sports car growl. A petrol pump kicked into life - the family man. Rebecca looked back towards her car. Bezzec was still inside, hidden by tricks of light and shadow. She prayed he would stay there.

It was cool and bright in the shop. Soft rock played. Rebecca spilled coins and notes onto the counter. Her hands shook. She glanced back through the window. The family man had finished filling his Rover estate. The van pulled away.

Behind the counter, a sullen middle-aged woman glared impatiently at Rebecca as she tried to count out the correct payment.

Another vehicle arrived.

Figures raced around the perimeter of the filling station.

Then in.

There was a shout of astonishment, the shout became a scream as three, no four of them, bounded across the forecourt. One scrambled up and over the family car. Its owner stumbled back, the pump nozzle still in his hand. Petrol sprayed in a great silvery arc onto the side of his car. The van screeched to a halt.

Rebecca froze.

The Cuthella hurtled towards the shop, mouths wide open, trailing ropes of saliva. All was screaming and shouting.

Beyond the approaching monsters, the door of her hatchback

61

swung open and Bezzec flowed out, all dislocated and distorted as he forced his vast bulk through the tiny gap. Engines roared, a horn blared and tyres squealed. A child shrieked, on and on. The van lurched into reverse.

And slammed into one of the Cuthella. It pitched sideways, skidded across the concrete on its back, limbs shattered and useless, head bouncing, until it smacked against the wheels of a customised Clio belonging to a near-hysterical youth who was huddled against its flanks screaming.

Bezzec loomed behind the remaining two Cuthella, one of which tumbled to an ungainly halt and began to turn. The closest, however, was out of Bezzec's reach. The closest threw itself at the shop window.

Rebecca finally managed to move, and began her own turn and flight.

Glass exploded and fury came in.

The Cuthella crashed into a shelf unit laden with crisps and sweets. The shelves overturned. The assistant shrieked. Rebecca staggered backwards, looking for a weapon. The Cuthella scuttered round, torn flesh hung from its skull, white pus-blood streamed over it eyes and dripped onto the floor. Its jaw hung open, its tiny chest heaved. It seemed dazed, hurt. The assistant's screaming, the tumult outside faded into the background, loud yet inconsequential at this moment.

Rebecca's hand closed round a can, she grabbed it and saw that it was hairspray. As she ripped off the plastic lid, the Cuthella launched itself at her. She rammed her fist onto the can's plunger. It hissed, the Cuthella squealed and threw itself sideways. It folded in on itself, clawed at its own eyes. Rebecca moved in, thumb hard on the plunger.

The door thudded open and Bezzec roared and the Cuthella's head disappeared under the hammer of his fist.

A moment later Bezzec had Rebecca's arm and was hauling her roughly towards her car. A growl bubbled from his mouth and the gathering crowd cowered back. Rebecca glimpsed Cuthella bodies. From somewhere a blue light strobed.

He forced her into the car, snarling in some language she couldn't understand. He wouldn't leave her alone, he forced her to do things, to scrabble the key at the ignition, to crash the car into gear.

"Fastly," Bezzec repeated. "Fastly, fastly!"

The car lurched forward then raced off the forecourt, narrowly missing the young lad who was still huddled beside his Clio.

Rebecca shouted and Bezzec roared as they careered towards a confusion of exits. Rebecca hit the accelerator and surged onto the roundabout. There were entrances to the Place everywhere. A swerve, a reckless lane-cross and she was on the slip-road she wanted.

Jonathon and Mary Samuels' bungalow was in darkness.

Rebecca parked the hatchback on the side of the road rather than in the driveway. Now she was crouched behind the high hedge that fronted the house while Bezzec carried out an initial check. She couldn't hear him. He was astonishingly light on his feet for someone so big.

"Lady," he rumbled softly.

Rebecca moved carefully out of her hiding place. Bezzec was standing on the drive, his back to the house. His huge fist was clenched, his snakelike neck fully uncoiled and restless.

The Samuels' car was parked in the drive. Its carefully polished paintwork glinted where moonlight touched. Bezzec waited as Rebecca rang the door bell. She heard its "Oranges and Lemons" warble, but there was no reply, no comforting lighting of lights, no amiable calls of "Coming, coming!" from Jonathon.

Another attempt and another. The front door itself was deadlocked and immovable.

"We'll have to go round the back," she told Bezzec.

He led the way down the side of the bungalow and round to the back door. Like Rebecca, the Samuels had a conservatory, added to a much older flat roof extension.

The orange aura that was Watford stained the sky beyond the fields.

Apart from the infra-red security light which flicked on as they rounded the corner, there was no illumination either inside or outside the house. Rebecca tried the conservatory door and was surprised to find it ajar. She glanced at Bezzec, whose head was close to her shoulder, then went in.

She fumbled around for the light switch.

The stillness was absolute and the silence roared as she led the way past the wicker furniture and potted plants into the kitchen.

Some of her scream escaped before she was able to silence herself.

Jonathon's eyes were open, his skin blue-black, his torso was so swollen the seams of his shirt had given way.

There was no humanity left. He was a grotesque doll, with rigid, puffy limbs that stuck out from an inflated imitation of a body

Rebecca stared because she could do nothing else. The she slumped down onto the nearest chair. It was the only one left standing in what she slowly realised was a devastated, kitchen. She began to cry. Bezzec's huge hand closed gently about her shoulder and his head curled round to regard her, an almost comical expression of concern on his miniature face.

"Cuthella and G'ein," he growled. "G'ein sting."

Mary was in the bedroom, which was virtually undisturbed. A rustle of curtain caught Rebecca's attention. The window was open.

Had Mary been asleep? She lay on top of the duvet, wearing her day clothes, stretched and torn as her body had blackened and swelled. An afternoon nap? Perhaps she felt unwell; the beginning of what should have been a quiet, natural death.

"David!" Rebecca's voice was absorbed by the silence. "David! DAVID!"

"Gone," said Bezzec. "Takun."

"Why didn't he create a Circle?" Rebecca demanded. "Why didn't he protect himself and his mother and father?"

"Suckles are rare."

"He should have taken it with him."

"Loves yuh I s'pose."

Rebecca took a dressing gown off the back of the bedroom door and laid it gently over Mary Samuels. Guilt was tearing at the fabric of her calm. This was a visitation from God upon those she loved. He did that in the bible didn't he? Yea unto generation and generation.

Exhausted and lost, Rebecca slumped onto the stool by Mary's dressing table. Bezzec remained by the door. She felt no fear of him anymore. There was that gentleness about him that could only come from something as big and strong as he was.

"We have to go into the Place don't we," Rebecca said.

Chapter Eleven

She made a telephone call first. They were parked on the hard shoulder of the M25, just short of an exit that had no junction number and, Rebecca knew, would not be marked on any map. Traffic rocked the car as it hurtled by.

"Rebecca? Oh thank Christ." Lynne sounded panic-stricken. "Where are you? Are you at home?"

"No," Rebecca answered carefully.

"Well don't go there...Or perhaps you should. Look, I've...I called the police. I was pissed off with you, I...I suppose I did it to get back at you. I told them everything, about your confession, everything. They're probably at the cottage now. I'm sorry." She began to cry, something Rebecca could not imagine.

"It's doesn't matter," Rebecca said as gently as she was able. "I just wanted to say that it's all okay."

"What are you going to do? Rebecca...Oh my God, don't - "

"I'm just...just keeping out of the way for a while." She paused, not knowing how to end the call. "Thanks Lynne, for everything." She cut the connection abruptly then switched off the phone.

So were they at the cottage yet, the lane filled with their cars, blue-stroboscopes tearing the darkness? Were they examining the torn front door, or crunching about the glass-strewn kitchen? Perhaps they were gathered round the BMW...

The hidden exit led onto a wide, straight road bordered by high hedges. So far it seemed normal, nothing flew over the car, the verges looked familiar enough and the surface under the hatchback's tyres felt smooth. Rebecca was beginning to wonder if Bezzec had made a mistake, when the Dali Elephants appeared.

She should have been prepared, should not been shocked when the car rounded a corner and its headlights picked out what looked like giant plant stems a hundred yards ahead. She hit the brakes and the car slewed to a halt. The plant stems moved. They were legs, insectile, advancing slowly into the cone of head light.

Something uncurled into the light. A tentacle, octopoid and complete with glistening flesh and suckers. The legs, closer now, reminded Rebecca of the grotesque limbs Salvador Dali gave to those surreal pachyderms of his.

"Dunt stup!" Bezzec yelled. "Go. Hurry!"

"But where?" Rebecca was already crunching the gears into reverse. The car lurched backwards.

"No, go forrids."

Forwards? Dear God she couldn't drive into those things –

"Forrids!"

Against every instinct, Rebecca's raced the car at the forest of legs and groping tentacles. She glimpsed shapes scrambling down the limbs in the last moments before she plunged into them. Cuthella, those things carried Cuthella...

Then she was ploughing through. The legs quivered and danced aside with astonishing agility, their owners obviously used to dodging potentially disastrous obstacles. A tentacle lashed again the metalwork, there was a bang, a scrape.

And they were clear, rushing down that long, hedge-lined road at a speed Rebecca had never dared attempt in her life. The hatchback's engine howled, the car bounced despite the smooth surface.

Ahead, a sharp corner wrenched the road to the right and out of sight. God knew what lay beyond it. As she began the turn Rebecca's mouth dried, she tensed, realised she was holding her breath –

The road, narrowed to a lane that speared between a jumble of stone cubes and rectangles. Buildings. It was a village. The street was illuminated by fiercely burning braziers mounted atop tall poles (wood, iron, Rebecca couldn't tell). The braziers burned blood-red and cast a hellish wash. The dwellings themselves were punctured by windows and doors. The doors were tight shut, the windows featureless black eyes.

"Who lives here?" Rebecca had to force herself to speak.

"Cast-Outs. Like me, afore I runned away to fight with the Libby Raider. Bad old places. Some friends, some enemies. Mustn't stup long. The Wuhman's childrens are everywhere."

"Mustn't stop? Did you say *stop?*"

"Yus, for foods and waters."

Rebecca shuddered, the village seemed endless, the black-eyed houses uncountable, crammed on both flanks of the hills that climbed away from the road and up into the darkness. Rebecca forced herself to relax, but within seconds the tension crept back. She wanted to drive faster, to get out of that place, but the road was too narrow, too rough.

"Stup. Here, stup."

She braked and in a moment was alone in the car. She had told

Bezzec to be careful. His bizarre baby-eyes had twisted back to stare at her and he had growled something that might have been thank you.

Rebecca left the engine running, but it was still like silence. She watched Bezzec hurry along the street. He stopped at one of the dwellings and pounded the door, which opened and spilled enough light for Rebecca to glimpse something that seemed to ooze rather than walk. It drew back inside. Bezzec followed.

Alone in the car.

This, Rebecca decided, was the very essence of alone. She glanced right, peered into the narrow strip of darkness between herself and the dwelling by which she had parked. Then behind, not trusting the mirror, then left, at the street, splashed by blood-glare and pooled with impenetrable shadow.

Something moved.

Snagged by her peripheral vision.

Nothing. The narrow street was an empty patchwork of light and shade.

Rebecca checked that the doors were locked. "Come *on* Bezzec, hurry up, please." All through gritted teeth.

Another full scan. Behind...perhaps...no, nothing. Right, that narrow deep gully walled with steel and stone. Ahead. There was something out there, hidden now by the car's bonnet. She re-checked the locks, slumped back in the seat and realised that she was still wearing her seat belt. How law-abiding she was.

Time for another scan of the street -

It boiled out of the shadows and up onto the bonnet.

Boiled, yes, a surging, heaving, roiling mass that glowed softly in the dark. Colours shifted inside its shapeless, writhing flesh.

Harmless, it was harmless okay, a Cast-Out like Bezzec, who was Hell with one arm, but also her friend.

Rebecca became aware that she had pressed herself against the back of the seat, transfixed by the slow progress of the creature as it slid over the bonnet and smeared itself across the windscreen.

The street was obscured by dingy rainbow shifts of light and the dimly viewed vessels and organs. A wide open mouth kissed the glass wetly. Rebecca went for the driver's door, but saw its arms, sliding across the glass. Stupid move, she had to stay here and not scream or cry and wait for Bezzec to come and rip the thing from the car.

She was safe. Everything was locked and sealed, it couldn't get in -

Softly glowing filaments, uncurled from between the slats of the driver-side air vents. More, up from the windscreen vents. She grabbed at the nearest, intending to tear them out. Hot pain drove into her right palm and she flinched back with a cry. The cry threatened to dissolve into hysteria. She bit down on the noise and held her injured hand to herself. More and more filaments emerged from the vents.

Carefully she levered herself up, then scrambled into the back in an ungainly clamber. She landed in a pile and lay there, not wanting to sit up anymore.

Light pulsed about her. She could hear slithering, sucking noises from outside. She realised that she was lying on the cardigan and quickly struggled it on. She zipped it up to her neck and turned up its collar, the action awkward because the fingers of her right hand had stiffened slightly. At least it would protect her arms and neck from the creature's stings.

The first of the filaments felt its way between the front seats.

Other filaments crept over the top of the driver's seat and groped towards her. She curled into a foetus position and covered her head with her arms.

And remembered Mary and Jonathon Samuels. Stung to death, swollen and blackened by poisons. Is this what killed them, this relentless, blindly groping horror? Dear God, she was going to die the way they did, was going to look like them...

Every window in the car was covered now. More filaments waved in from the edges of the rear doors. She slid into the gap between the rear seat and the driver's seat and pulled the coat over her head. Her arms ached, the stings burned, every movement was an effort.

The car was filling up with the thing's lethal, hair-thin feelers, they were slowly, inexorably stretching towards her. Even here, in the muffled, cloth-smelling dark she could sense them as they explored the folds of thick material, looking for gaps.

The hatchback rocked violently. It was crushing the car, Dear Jesus, any moment now glass would shatter and in it would pour –

Another shudder, a roar, a noise like the tearing of fabric.

There was a final violent lurch then a cacophony of sound outside. Silence followed. No, the car shook again. She coiled herself more tightly. Something touched her. She screamed, the sound muffled by the coat.

"Lady, are yuh well?"

Chapter Twelve

Avy's house was a place of asymmetrical geometries, bare, walls and a web-like spiral of gantries that led off a central pillar. The house itself was a narrow tower formed from an irregular polygon. Everything in Avy's house was irregular, the central pillar itself was curved into a long, shallow 'C'.

Rebecca lay on the flat upper edge of one of the gantries, about halfway to the top, which was a softly glowing dome. The gantry seemed to be made of a tightly weaved fibre, whether natural or not she couldn't tell. The source of the glow was invisible to her, not that she cared. She was too ill to wonder at the eccentricities of this place.

The wounds in her right palm were a scatter of pinpricks circled in angry red. Whatever poison they had given entrance to, had paralysed her.

She wanted to scream, but the sound was locked inside her, trapped in a nerve-dead, useless, useless body that wouldn't answer her. Nothing would react or even exist. She was awareness only, a glow of consciousness adrift on a sea of utter, terrible, nothingness.

Bezzec had carried her from the car, cradled her in his single arm and dragged himself up the central pillar by his feet. The journey, an upside down swing and lurch, was terrifying. But she was here now, supine and staring up at another strangeness.

Avy.

Bezzec had called her that, *her* because there was something about the glistening flow of tissue and colour that suggested femininity. Avy was… reptile perhaps, lizard, chameleon even, with long, delicate toes. Her head was a soft-toned wedge, inset with two large, dark and featureless eyes. Unlike a lizard, her mouth was not a pair of long, grinning jaws, but a lipless, ever-changing hole at the end of her snout.

Avy's voice was a soft chirrup, punctuated by delicate sighs and murmurs that sounded bizarrely human. At this moment she clung to a narrow gantry two levels up from where Rebecca lay and Bezzec stood guard.

He was looking up at Avy and growling in a language that Rebecca had never heard before. Avy whispered and sighed in return. At last, Bezzec's neck arced downwards and he returned his attention to Rebecca.

"You need to be welled," he said.

Yes, she did, she most definitely needed to be welled.

"I ull go to the Wellmakers."

No, Rebecca shouted to him silently, and that silence was a horror because it completed her helplessness. No Bezzec, don't leave me here with her. Send Avy. Please Bezzec she can go can't she -

Bezzec stared at her for a moment longer and through the red-haze of her agonies and fear, Rebecca realised that his eyes were almost identical to Avy's. Then he grunted, swung round and was gone, no doubt swinging from gantry to gantry using those astonishing prehensile feet of his.

Rebecca could still breathe, though it took an immense effort. Each inhalation and exhalation had to be planned and forced. This then was what it had been like for Mary and Jonathon, only worse. Oh God...

She forced the panic down, crushed it and was astonished by the strength of her will.

Avy moved. For a moment she disappeared into the mesh of gantries then reappeared lower down. Rebecca watched, helpless and afraid. Soft as Avy's eyes were, she was still reptile, utterly alien and incomprehensible.

Her movements were careful, graceful, catlike.

Avy settled onto a gantry directly above Rebecca. She stared, until the stare became uncomfortable. Then her head began to descend, her neck elongated. Rebecca wanted to roll over, get away, scream, anything. She couldn't of course. She dragged breath painfully into her lungs.

Avy's face dissolved, became tentacles that uncoiled and stretched. Rebecca sank back into herself as the tentacles touched her, became an embrace then a gentle exploration of the landscape of her face.

Such a likeness.

The voice shivered through her, silent yet no thought of her own.

The statement didn't make sense.

Rebecca experienced fear, but, like the voice, it was not her own.

The tentacles withdrew, Avy's face reformed and she withdrew to a higher gantry where she settled herself and became motionless...No, not completely motionless, her body moved...rippled. Rebecca watched, but could make out no details.

Inhale...exhale...she couldn't close her eyes. She wanted to close her eyes. She steadied her breathing. Inhale...Exhale.

A dull vibration shuddered through the gantry. A moment, then Bezzec clawed himself into view, feet first.

He stood awkwardly, his body sheened in sweat. There were other

70

fluids splashed over him, an ominous sign. He was alone. No Wellmakers, dear God, no one to *well* her from this horror of numbness and pain.

"Know we's here," he grunted. "Havtuh go fastly." He turned and uttered a string of growls and snarls.

Knows? Who knows?

Wings whirred and a stream of shapes spiralled into Rebecca's line of sight.

Sajanath. The same creatures she had seen on that day when David had told her about the Place. "They're not very bright and they don't grant wishes." That's what he had told her. Bright or not, these ones had purpose, and if it was malevolent, there was nothing she could do about it.

They closed in, their tiny faces screwed into expressions of intense concentration. The first of them landed on the gantry beside Rebecca's injured hand. It dropped to its knees, leaned over the sting-site and opened its mouth. A long proboscis unrolled from inside and dipped into the one of the wounds.

It drank, for ten, twenty seconds then jerked back.

Its wings…Oh God, its wings shrivelled, its face blackened, then, body arched impossibly backwards, it was thrown into convulsions. Rebecca cried out, the sound little more than a tortured groan. The fact that she was able to speak at all was lost in grief as the Sajanath crumpled into a dry-looking husk then became dust, scattered by the wing beat of another of the creatures. Without hesitation, the second Sajanath repeated the operation until it too shrivelled and died.

Another took its place and another.

As the eighth Sajanath faded to dust, Rebecca managed to sit up. There was desperation in the act. She had to prove that she was healed so that the sacrifice could stop.

The surviving Sajanath swirled upwards to dance about her head for a moment then they were gone, lost in the incomprehensible dimensions of Avy's house.

David had been wrong about them. Ignorance, or a lie?

"Lady, are yuh well?" That familiar question. Rebecca had only known Bezzec for a day or so and already he felt like an old friend.

"Why did they have to die?"

"To defeat thuh Woman," Bezzec said. "Munny havta die."

This was a real war wasn't it, where people – Cast-Outs, call them what you will – died. But why was *she* so important that these creatures

71

had to die for her? She, Rebecca was just an interloper, interfering in this life-and-death struggle as she searched for a man who shouldn't exist and who she didn't know if she even loved -

A squeal, pig-like, another familiarity.

Rebecca started, looked up at Bezzec. His neck arced towards her, his eyes blinked then he looked up and snarled another request, order, plea. For a moment Rebecca thought it was aimed at her, then realised that he was talking to Avy.

More squeals and snuffles. Rebecca peered down through the branch-like spirals of gantries and flinched back, unable to breathe, unable to comprehend the utter desperation of the situation.

There were Cuthella down there, ascending the gantries with the ease of apes. Scores of them, hundreds even.

Another sentence from Bezzec, and movement from above.

Cuthella… No, a figure. Avy… not Avy.

Rebecca.

Her.

Even the clothes were identical, jeans, a black zip-up sweater.

Oh God, Avy had become *her.*

She dropped onto the gantry where Rebecca and Bezzec waited. She looked at Rebecca for a moment and Rebecca saw that what looked back at her through Avy's eyes was not her. It was powerful, and ancient. And utterly, immeasurably calm.

Rebecca noticed that the clothes were unstable. They…pulsed, vessels, blood, just visible, weaved into wool and cotton that wasn't wool and cotton at all. The effect was of one of instability, as if Avy's mimicry was fragile, short-lived.

"I can give you time, but little else," Avy said. Hearing her own voice was even more unnerving to Rebecca than seeing her face.

Avy turned to Bezzec and gently, tenderly, touched his chest, just above his mouth. His huge hand covered hers. There was an exchange, silent but deep then Avy broke away and before Rebecca could cry out or make any attempt to stop her, leapt over the edge.

Rebecca's last glimpse her was of her landing with catlike grace on a lower gantry. Then she leapt again, the Cuthella in pursuit.

"We havtuh go lady. Fastly go." Bezzec.

Inertia, the inability to think or move because Rebecca knew that Avy had just sacrificed herself. Another death on her hands.

It mustn't be wasted.

It couldn't be wasted.

Joints aching, thoughts slow, Rebecca nodded and let Bezzec hoist her onto his shoulders. She clung on, closed her eyes, felt like a child, secure in Bezzec's care.

They went upwards.

Bezzec hauled himself from gantry to gantry with his one huge arm, finding footholds in the matted fibres of the gnarled central column when the gantries became further apart. Rebecca glanced over her shoulder, more afraid of Cuthella than of the height. No sign of them. They must have taken the bait.

Yet.

The roof was a dome of stained glass. As Bezzec carried her closer, Rebecca saw –

That the images in the glass.

Were of her.

Of Rebecca Ann Samuels. Her wedding. Her baptism, standing beside Pastor Emerson in the water in front of the pulpit in Abbotsfield Baptist chapel. Her naked body, entwined with David, *Dr* David. She knew it was Dr David and not…*David*, And there she was, caught in mid-whirl, hair splayed, face wrenched into shock from a blow.

Inevitably, she could be seen, standing over his crumpled body, and his time there was a hammer in her hand.

The roof of Avy's house was a huge, glass-fleshed, spiral tapestry of her life.

That ended with a machine, its borders lost in the maelstrom of images. At its centre, bound and pierced, spread-armed, by its cablery and pipework, was a woman.

Rebecca.

More disturbing still, the machine crucifix was flanked on either side by a naked figure of David Samuels.

"Down look!" Bezzec roared.

Rebecca obeyed.

And saw Cuthella, still some way down but gaining fast. Avy's deceit had either failed or she was dead.

The roof exploded, startling Rebecca in a shower of multi-coloured shards. Still looking down she saw great jagged fragments bounce and shatter on the lower gantries. A Cuthella was hit, the impact pitching the creature into space, overlong arms flailing.

Bezzec was bleeding. Two huge gashes were torn into the arm he had obviously used as a sledgehammer to break through the ceiling.

Rebecca shouted some vague question about whether he was all right, but her words failed as they clawed out onto the roof.

The night had turned red. The air was drenched with smoke.

The town was burning, great pillars of smoke and flame coiled skywards. There was noise too, the crackle of conflagration mingled with shouts, screams and roars. Things circled, darted between the smoke columns, leather-winged, tailed...

Something flew over the car. . .

All this because Rebecca Ann Samuels was here?

Rebecca wavered under the idea that such destruction and carnage was taking pace because of her. There must be another reason. She as an innocent bystander that was it, a traveller inadvertently caught up in someone else's war. Who, purely by coincidence of course, had her biography and martyrdom illustrated in glass.

Martyrdom? That was it had looked like, Rebecca the crucified Messiah.

Perhaps she should give herself up.

The thought was like a thorn, snagged in her mind.

Perhaps she should surrender herself and accept whatever horror it involved as punishment for her crime. She was a murderer after all and they used to hang murderers didn't they? And how many times had she, quietly, wished cruel retribution on other stealers of human life?

One of the surreal elephant creatures emerged from the smoke. Rebecca saw that its body was not elephantine at all, but vaguely spherical, membranous sacs adorned with tentacles, the main purpose of which seemed to be loading and discharging their cargoes of Cuthella.

The elephant creature closed in, stepping between the walls of Cast Out dwellings. A handful of Cuthella clung to its soft, pulsing body. Something howled and screeched from out of the shattered glass behind Rebecca, a reminder that she and Bezzec were trapped..

Bezzec grabbed her, the action startling. "Hold hud lady!"

The Cuthella leapt.

Bezzec leapt.

Rebecca glimpsed Cuthella as they crossed in mid-jump. Then the soft-glowing, vein-laced flesh of the elephant thing's flesh rushed towards, and slammed into, her.

She rolled free and grabbed at the soft, dank membrane. A figure rose up in front of her. Bezzec... no, a Cuthella. It hissed, lashed out with its ludicrous arm. Rebecca flinched back, surprised by the speed of her reaction. She glanced about for Bezzec. No sign of him. The elephant thing lurched and swayed under her. The Cuthella slashed at her again, another flinch back then Rebecca drove herself at the Cuthella's shrunken torso, arms extended, feet slipping despite the stickiness of the elephant-thing's flesh.

She felt, not saw, the impact, heard the Cuthella's howl, opened eyes she had not realised were closed and saw the creature fall away into the fire-painted dark. There was a moment of anguish, of guilt, but only a moment.

Bezzec lumbered over the rise of the elephant creature's body. At his urging, Rebecca clambered onto his back once more. A tentacle curled upwards, fluids ebbed and flowed beneath its translucent flesh. Bezzec grasped the limb as it lashed overhead and Rebecca was thrown into space.

She screamed, closed her eyes and tightened her grip. The descent ripped her stomach up through her body. At some point Bezzec jumped free to make a hard landing. Rebecca let go and collapsed onto her hands and knees. Roaring and snarling, Bezzec jerked her to her feet. She saw her car. Her strength failed.

Bezzec dragged her to the hatchback and released her long enough to wrench open the driver's door then hurry round to the other side of the car. She stared at him, made helpless by shock and fear. Bezzec's neck swung round, eyes reflecting the shifting red of the fire.

"In." A soft growl, his version of gentleness.

Rebecca heard, but couldn't respond. She was tired, everything ached.

"In Lady. *Lady!*" His roar shook her enough to get into the car. Bezzec clambered in beside her. She grabbed at the key, twisted it. The engine coughed, struggled.

Gears… which was first? A crunch, grind, a kangaroo jerk and they were away. Rebecca slammed her right foot hard down. The street rushed at her, a billow of smoke, its stink filled the car. Figures, Cuthella, looped across her path.

And a wall. A giant black wave surging down the street, a shifting impenetrable nothingness.

There was no time to stop. No time to think or feel fear.

As the hatchback slammed into the dark.

Rebecca had expected a final impact, a violence that would rip her apart in a brief moment of pain and madness.

There was nothing, no sensation, no impact or violence, only -

Darkness.

Solid and impenetrable.

Physical enough to shallow her breathing, to press against her eyes, to dislodge spirit from body and set it afloat.

From somewhere distant she felt the rim of the car's steering wheel under her hands. The engine hummed, a vague whirr in the background. A connection. She clung to it, focussed on it.

The claustrophobia flooded back.

She needed light, grey even, anything but this suffocating, cloying, blackness.

Even *that* light, the dim glow ahead. A warm, comforting glow. She swung the wheel towards it.

Bezzec grabbed her arm in his immense fist. "Nuh," he said quietly. Startled, Rebecca pulled the wheel left and the light slid out of view.

You know Becky. How she hated being called Becky. *I don't think you have any idea just how attractive you are.*

He, James Bayfield, touched her hair, brushed it gently from her face then trailed his work-roughened fingertips over her cheek, to her lips.

Rebecca recoiled, her cry of shock muffled by the dark.

Bayfield? Here?

Behind her, leaning over the seat to play with her hair.

Hello Becky. His accent was upper-class correct, his tone authoritative, but never arrogant or aggressive. There was a blurred edge to it tonight, and a flavour to his breath.

Alcohol.

Night fleshed hands slid over her shoulders and down to her breasts.

Stung by revulsion, sixteen years old again, Rebecca jerked her foot down hard on the accelerator. Run away screamed her young self, don't let him touch you.

His night hands were running over her abdomen, rough and hard.

Why did you set the police on me Becky? Hmmmm? Silly little bitch. Why did you run away? We could have had a lot of fun -

Hands all over her, pulling at her clothes, her hair.

She screamed, thrashed her head from side to side, hauled at the steering wheel and pointed the car towards the light. Oh, the light...

Someone else was roaring at her. She ignored them, she had to escape from *him*, from his hands, from the brutal pain that burrowed between her tight-clenched thighs, from his stinking alcoholic breath and his vile whispering.

Light, light, had to get to the light.

It swirled out of the dark, a vast gleaming whirlpool that shifted through the spectrum, red to violet, beautiful enough to make her cry, an offer of cleansing. Bayfield swarmed over her, his lips snuffling for hers as he groped and clawed and poured hot breath into her ear.

She liked it didn't she? This rough handling.

No, she hated it.

And you Bayfield. I hate you. . .

Rebecca. . . Rebecca. . . REBECCA!

Bezzec's roar smashed through the black. Startled, she swung the steering wheel to the left.

The car plunged on into the light.

Which expanded and became.

A mouth.

The car shuddered and roared as the front was dragged up some unseen hill. Bayfield grunted in triumph and Rebecca gasped as she felt him penetrate her, big and barbed. The friction was agony. She bit her lip, clenched the rim of the wheel and the car hurtled round the perimeter of the vast, blazing mouth.

Things spiralling out of the light, winged, tailed and familiar.

Something flew over the car. . .

The car lurched and tumbled. Rebecca burned as Bayfield pounded into her.

And she was out, racing along the street.

There were flames, smoke, the gangling, awkward canter of Cuthella, and other figures, odd, inhuman. Fighting, Rebecca knew, for their lives.

For her.

A Dali elephant hove into view; spindle legs, waving tentacles. Rebecca reacted on instinct. She swerved, almost hit a house, careered back into the centre of the road and hurtled through the elephant's legs.

Then there was only night.

Chapter Thirteen

There was forest on the far side of the village. The road itself became progressively rougher, its surface broken by the roots of the trees and other giant plants.

Rebecca knew she shouldn't be driving. She was injured, exhausted, her concentration wavered.

"Yuh doin' gud," Bezzec growled every fifteen minutes or so.

Each time she returned the encouragement.

It became a litany.

Bezzec emitted a gruff coughing sound that she realised was probably a chuckle. They reached a junction. The forest road was a maze of them. Bezzec never hesitated in choosing a direction.

"What is this woman like?" Rebecca wondered why she needed to know. Was she jealous perhaps?

"Yuh," Bezzec answered.

"Me? How can she be like me?"

"She is yuh."

"Is... me?" She frowned. Her hand throbbed and was difficult to curl round the steering wheel.

"Ah."

"But I don't know anything about the Place. I've never been there...Not for any length of time." She subsided. She was missing the point wasn't she?

No, she was trying to *avoid* the point.

Another junction. "Luft," grunted Bezzec.

"Do you mean that she's human like me?" Something dark and unthinkable was uncoiling itself in the cellar of her mind. "That's what you mean isn't it."

Please Bezzec, say "Ah."

"Neh." No, she supposed. He had never said no before.

"She is yuh."

"The..." She swallowed, difficult with a dry mouth. "The real Rebecca Ann Samuels?" No, she would be Rebecca Wright wouldn't she.

"Ah," Pleased, like a teacher who has finally got some point through to a particularly dense child.

The Woman is the real Rebecca, the human Rebecca. Me? I'm... Oh fuck. The word didn't help this time. Oh fuck, oh fuck. I'm a Changeling.

Like Dr Samuels. A second rate impostor. Something moulded in some vat of organic slime. Not real. Not *me*. That dowdy weirdo who really is a dowdy weirdo. And if my parents ever met this Woman, would their eyes mist over and would they rush to smother her in the love they had never seemed able to fully give to their substitute daughter?

And the real me? The real Rebecca? A hated, vicious dictator?

Oh shit, oh God, oh dear Jesus.

I'm a Changeling.

A Change-Eh-Ling.

Just like Dr David Samuels.

Something dropped onto the car.

Ran down the widescreen, gelatinous, faintly glowing, mouth caressing the glass.

G'ein.

Another impact. Rebecca accelerated, as if, somehow, it would save them. Instead the world became a chaos of all-but uncontrollable swerves as the speeding car bounced and careered over the broken roadway.

Filaments were already sprouting from the air vents. From the gaps round the doors.

Bezzec yelled for her to stop. She screamed back at him that she couldn't. He grabbed the steering wheel and the car was yanked to the left. The shuddering became a tumult. Rebecca instinctively lifted her right foot and rammed it onto the brake. Bezzec tore open his door, clamped his huge hand on Rebecca's arm and wrenched her, bumping and struggling over the handbrake, onto the passenger seat and out onto the ground.

He jerked her to her feet. She leaned on him, barely able to stand. The car glowed, a mass of G'ein flesh.

"Go. Forrids." He pointed down the road. "Thut way. Go! Get to the little chuch!"

She stumbled back from him, confused. "But you're coming with me. Bezzec, what are you talking about?"

"Go," he repeated. "Go. Go!"

Still she hesitated.

A Cuthella screeched, from the darkness on the other side of the road. Another, another. Sticks snapped, there was movement, fast, awkward bounding, shadows raced towards them. It was an ambush.

"GO!" Bezzec roared. "THAT WAY, FORRIDS. GO!"

And the first of the Cuthella leapt, snarling, out of the dark.

Her last sight of Bezzec was of his great arm, its flesh ripped and hanging in shreds as he used it to break Cuthella skulls. There were too many for him...

When she finally stumbled out of the forest, dawn had prised the sky from the horizon and the first pink hues were showing through the wound. She was breathless, dazed. She had been running for hours, minutes, she couldn't tell. It was all a confusion of fear, grief and exhaustion.

First there had been the headlong stumble away for the car, paralleling the road, a blind rush over fallen boughs and lashing branches, on and on until she had careered into a huge tree. The trunk was warm, something like a heartbeat thrummed deep inside it. She slumped to the ground and wept herself to sleep.

Sounds woke her, the crash of living things over the forest floor, the squeals of Cuthella, distant, but closing in.

She ran again, bleary from sudden awakening, plunged deeper into the confusion of plants and trees; forrids, always forrids. And suddenly she had burst into the clear.

The ground, which was rich in plants and tall grass and alive with Sajannath, sloped away from her towards a road she recognised as one of the lanes that led into Abbotsfield. There was a corn field between the edge of the Place and the road. The harvest was complete, the corn now stubble littered with straw bales. Abbotsfield itself was about a mile or so to the left, the church tower just visible on the far horizon.

A long, mournful cry sounded and was answered by another.

Startled, she glanced left and saw a Dali Elephant striding towards her along the forest edge. The creature was still some way off and in no hurry. A glance to the right revealed two more even further away, but advancing as inexorably as their companion. Great insect limbs thudded into the soft ground, the fleshy orb atop them swayed and its tentacles groped blindly.

Cuthella scuttled down its legs.

To Abbotsfield then, although he village would be swarming with police. Perhaps she should wait until dark.

A Cuthella screech stopped that idea.

She was trapped. Please God, she begged as she set off down the slope, if they catch me, at least let them kill me, quickly. She did not want to be taken prisoner.

Rebecca broke into a breathless, panic-powered run. She drove herself through long, dew-drenched grass and did not, dare not, look back.

She almost stumbled straight into a G'ein.

It was spread across her path, concealed by the grass that surrounded it. Rebecca veered left. Filaments lashed out at her and she manoeuvred herself out of its reach so violently she almost fell. *That would have been death*, she panted to herself, over and over again, using the chant to push her on through the grass and out into the stubble field.

Even then she kept running, focussed on the road, sobbing for breath, lungs burning. There was a gateway, closer, closer.

Then she was through and staggering to a halt on the grey tarmac. Birds, scavenging from a road-slaughtered rabbit, took flight and startled Rebecca with their violent wing-flaps and sudden movement.

Leaning forward, hands on knees, gasping air, she looked back. The field rolled up to its hedge-lined horizon. There was no sign of the Place, or of her pursuers.

Relief was subdued by the fact that there were other pursuers in this *place*, people who would be very interested to speak to Rebecca Samuels.

As soon as she had enough breath, Rebecca set of towards Abbotsfield. If a police car appeared she would have little time, or means, to hide herself, but the lane was the only route available so she no other choice.

The sun dragged itself higher, the fresh morning air warmed slightly. It was going to be a beautiful day.

Bezzec wouldn't see it.

The thought of him threatened to overwhelm her. She forced the memory down to some deep storeroom in her mind. There would be time enough to injure herself on its sharp edges.

Abbotsfield was silent and still when she reached its borders.

Rebecca approached as carefully as she could, walking along the pavement that took her past the windowless, crumbling side wall of the Old School. The lane opened out into a square known as the Plain. To her right was the Coach and Horses, directly opposite was the parish church, protected by its wrought iron gates and attended by moss-green grave stones.

The little chuch she supposed, though it was far from little.

The only cars she saw were parked and empty. Most curtains were drawn. She made to step away from the Old School. A police car swept into view. Suddenly there, sliding down the main street, its engine a whisper.

Rebecca flinched back, tensed. There were two exits out of the Plain. If the car took this one she was finished.

A moment, another, the engine sound faded. The car had taken the other route out of the Plain. She chuckled then bit down on the sound. Laughter, like tears would be hard to control.

A steadying breath, a whispered prayer then she broke out of her hiding place and made for the church. Seconds felt like hours, yards like miles, but she made the gates without incident.

They were locked.

So how did she get into the chuch? What was supposed to be there anyway? She gripped the gate's ironwork and tried to remember if there was another way in.

Engine.

Panicked, she looked round to see a lorry following the route taken by the police car. It was okay though, the police didn't drive lorries. It grew large, gears changed. As she watched its approach, Rebecca noticed the Happy Shopper, and beyond that the Baptist chapel. The Baptist *Church*, smaller than the parish one.

A *little chuch* in fact.

Chapter Fourteen

A woman with a blue halo sat in one of Abbotsfield Chapel's highly-polished, Pledge-scented pews. Her fair hair was long and fine and although she sat with her back to Rebecca, she was familiar. Disorientated, Rebecca paused by the doors, which, surprisingly, had been unlocked.

Rebecca needed to be careful. The woman might be a volunteer cleaner, or one of Emerson's three ruddily healthy and wholesome daughters back from Bible College or University.

The figure twisted round in the seat.

"Hello Mrs Samuels," she said and as she stood up Rebecca was startled to see that it was Tina, the receptionist from the village surgery, the petite and pretty young woman who had pushed her to the front of the queue in the waiting room and told her Dr Samuels was expecting her when Dr Samuels should have been dead.

"It's alright. I'm a friend." Tina lifted a candle from the pew beside her. The flame burned cold sapphire, the source of the aura that surrounded her. "You're safe in here. We have a Circle."

Tina waited as Rebecca walked up the aisle, the same aisle she had traversed on her wedding day. Early morning light gleamed through the chapel's high windows, pushing into, but not clearing the darkness. Despite the blue candle and the sheer strangeness of this meeting, Tina seemed so...normal. She wore a white blouse and black skirt, her receptionist's uniform. Her smile was a patient-reassuring, receptionist's smile.

"Is one alone?" A different voice, high pitched, childlike. It belonged to a second figure that uncurled from the gloom behind the pulpit.

It was big, hulking, and for a moment Rebecca thought...No, the rotund, bulging figure wasn't Bezzec, and never would be. It lumbered around the pulpit and stood over her. This Cast Out wore an immense boiler suit, had two arms and a head that accommodated eyes, ears and mouth. The head, however, was tiny, looking as if it belonged to a separate, diminutive being that had become trapped, neck-deep, in a swamp of living blubber.

"Drive." He introduced himself in that alarmingly high-pitched, fluting voice. His diction was beautiful. "At your service."

"I am alone," Rebecca said. "There was...I'm sorry." She felt as if it was her fault, and then realised that it probably was. Everything in the Place seemed to be her fault.

"Oh my," Drive said. "Poor dear Bezzec." He rubbed at his minute eyes with a vast hand then straightened. "Well, we must soldier on, isn't that right Tina."

"Yes Drive, you're right as always."

"Now, I think we should go down to the refuge, the holyman who owns this establishment will be here very soon. He likes to commune with his god early in the day you see."

Pastor Emerson the holyman, the title, though true, was an odd one. He had always seen himself as a shepherd, and he certainly didn't own the chapel. But what did it matter?

"You are very tired my dear," Drive said. "Allow me to carry you."

Too tired to protest, Rebecca let him scoop her into his arms. His body was soft, no hard muscle, just malleable fat that seem to mould itself about her. There was a door behind the pulpit, located in a shadowed alcove, never seen by her before and probably never noticed by Pastor Emerson, or any of his predecessors, or their congregations.

Beyond the door, stairs spiralled downwards, wooden at first, then stone. Tina led the way. She carried the blue candle and it cast just enough, unsteady light for Rebecca to see that the plain brick walls were engraved with symbols, each fragment briefly illuminated by the candle, and all incomprehensible.

There were smells; damp, musk, perfumes, incense perhaps.

At the bottom was another door, this one bigger, wider, some ten feet high, four or five feet wide its surface as smooth as the walls.

It gave onto a large, high-roofed, and reasonably well-lit room.

People waited.

The light was supplied by a brazier that burned with the same bloody light as those in the town Rebecca had come to think of as Avy's village .

Avy, another martyr.

Drive laid Rebecca gently onto the floor where she sat, hugging her arms and trembling.

"Rebecca." It was a woman, elderly by the sound of her voice. When she stepped into the light Rebecca saw that she was tall, slender and wore a high-collared, floor-length dress. Edwardian, Rebecca decided, although like so much in the Place, the comparison was approximate. The woman's long black-grey hair hung over the front of her left shoulder. Her face was hard. There was no warmth in either her voice or persona.

"Elabeth," Tina explained. "Our leader."

"And follower of the Liberator," Elabeth finished for her. The other figures stirred in the blood light and in the shadows; a sphere with a human face but no limbs, a dog like creature, broad shouldered, obviously accustomed to standing on its hind legs, something winged, with two heads, each tiny yet beautifully featured, a snake, with a woman's' head. Eyes lined its flanks. There were many others, the limits of the crowd blurred into the dark edges of the room.

"Bezzec," Rebecca managed, feeling she had to get this said first. "He...he died."

Elabeth nodded. There was murmuring. For a moment Rebecca wondered if they were going to attack her. But the murmuring faded. "A lot of us are going to die." Elabeth said. "Bezzec isn't the first, he won't be the last."

Rebecca wondered how she had managed to emerge as the leader of these creatures. There seemed little charisma about her. Her voice was cold, and edged with something that sounded like despair.

"I don't want anyone else to die for me. " Rebecca was shocked by her own assertiveness. She didn't know these p. She was never aggressive towards the people she knew, let alone strangers, especially those who were barely, and in many cases, not, human.

"This is a war," Elabeth said flatly. She looked down, a gesture that spoke of unfathomable sadness. "The war of the Woman."

"I'm here to find David, the Liberator." Libby Raider. Rebecca crushed a surge of grief.

"Then you are at war."

Rebecca wavered as dizziness washed through her. Drive was there, and exhausted, she slumped into his arms.

She woke with that initial sense of well-being that all awakenings gave her. That second or two of contentment, uncluttered by thoughts or fears or any grasp of the realities full consciousness would bring.

Panic followed close on its heels.

She scrabbled at the covers and tried to sit up. The room was ill-lit, the ceiling low and plagued by restless shadows.

A hand came to rest on her forehead and she twisted round to see Elabeth. She was startled. She had expected Tina, and Elabeth frightened her. The woman however was seated by the bed, sitting forward on the edge of a wooden chair that looked suspiciously like one of the long discarded wooden chairs from the chapel hall. The room was generally bare. But for a small table on which there stood a jug and bowl and the candles that provided the light.

"This is strange," Elabeth said gently. "To see you here."

"The Changeling Rebecca you mean, Rebecca the Second-Rate." Rebecca was surprised at her own venom.

"Ah, Bezzec told you."

"Yes. I'm sorry that he's dead. He was a good...a good man."

"Help us and his death will have meaning."

"I don't understand." Oh yes she did. And what was forming in her mind was terrifying.

"You can get us into the Woman's House."

No, that's what she wanted to say. I can't do anything like that. I couldn't pretend to be -

"The Woman has destroyed what once was a balanced world. The Cuthella, the G'ein and all the other horrors roam our corners of the world, because of her."

And Bezzec was prepared to die for whatever freedom these people were fighting for.

"I don't have a choice do I." The words felt like a death sentence.

Elabeth smiled. She was as beautiful as she was ancient. The smile was tight, however, and steeped in tragedy. For a moment her hand rested on Rebecca's cheek. Her flesh was cold, like ice, or that death Rebecca was anticipating.

"I suppose you know about...about what I did to my husband?"

Elabeth nodded. "There are times when we need to fight back. That was your time, this is our time."

Rebecca realised that she was disappointed that Elabeth offered no comfort or justification for her crime. But then, why should she?

A sound, muffled, from somewhere above the ceiling. Rebecca rolled onto her back and stared upwards. She strained to hear, could just make out a melody, familiar, possibly "Amazing Grace", but she couldn't be sure.

"Those people worship what they don't understand."

"Is that coming from the chapel?"

"Yes."

Rebecca tried to remember what day it was. Thursday, Thursday night was prayer meeting night at Abbotsfield Baptist chapel. Thursday *night?* She had arrived here early this morning and had slept all day. And if it was the prayer meeting, her mother and father would be there. All she had to do was scramble back up those narrow spiral stairs, run to them and hold them. She wanted them to take her home and succour her.

But they wouldn't do that would they? They would be appalled, horrified, afraid of their crazed daughter.

"What don't they understand?"

"What the gods are."

"Players of games."

Elabeth smiled again. "And the Place of course. It is the Place that they mistake for the presence of God in their midst."

The hymn ended. Rebecca lay motionless, hands splayed beside her on the mattress, trying to hear Pastor Emerson, whose voice was a smile.

"Good evening everyone. Shall we seek our Father's face in prayer?" He always asked it as question. Had anyone ever said no? Never, because he ruled this church with a rod of iron. His smile was also steel.

There was a sound that could have been a general "Amen" then the piano led them into another hymn. "What a friend we have in Jesus…"

Rebecca cried. The tune was evocative of simpler times. Or were they? Had she been happy, smothered as she was by the strictures of her mother's possessiveness, by her family's religion and by their desperate fight to remain respectable.

I'm a murderer now, she called out silently through the blank barrier of the ceiling. Your daughter, who isn't your daughter at all, is a murderer. Your real daughter is worse.

The hymn ended. There was a mumble that would be a scripture reading then more as Pastor Emerson settled into the usual half hour Bible study.

Prayers would follow, members of the congregation rising to plead with the Game Players for themselves and for the world. At some moment during that interminable mumble of voices her own father would stand and offer his own supplications to his God.

Much later, Tina brought food, packet curry and rice, purchased apparently, in the Happy Shopper next door and heated in the microwave in the chapel hall. There was also a cup of tea.

"I still don't understand how this Place works," Rebecca said as Tina perched herself on the edge of the bed. "Why don't you leave, escape into my…Place?"

"The borders are guarded by Cuthella and their like. And your people wouldn't accept us."

"*You* could escape though. You're –"

"No, I'm not human. I can get away with short spells in your Place, but that's all. You wouldn't want to know what I am."

"But what about the People themselves? Why don't they intervene?"

Tina laughed scornfully, the sound at odds with her persona. "The People!"

"You'll see Rebecca, in a few hours time."

Hours? She was still weak, disorientated. She needed days, not hours.

"We plan to assault the Woman's House tonight." Tina got to her feet. "The last of the fighters are still arriving. Get some rest. I'll be back to fetch you when the time comes." She paused, turned to stare at Rebecca with an intensity Tina the Receptionist would never have been able to achieve. "Just trust us Rebecca," she said. "No matter what happens."

She left, quickly, before Rebecca had time to respond.

Rebecca tried to force a forkful of curry into her mouth. It turned to mush on her tongue. Hours Tina had said, hours until she was pitched into some furious, violent nightmare she could not begin to imagine.

Defeated, Rebecca placed the plate on the chair by her bed then swung her legs out from under the blanket. A wave of nausea swept through her and she waited miserably until it was over.

Clothes had been folded and left on the end of the bed. After a moment, Rebecca snagged and drew them to herself. She struggled into a summer dress and saw that there was a sweater as well. It wasn't cold but it was comforting to wear somehow. She stood and waited out another wave of faintness before taking a step toward the table where the jug and bowl waited. The journey was a long one, but by the time she had reached her destination and washed her face she felt stronger and more alert. There was a towel which she used to dry herself. She ran her hands through her hair in an effort to straighten it out a little. Then she leaned on the table, dizzy again.

Something changed.

In the air, in the material of the reality around her, a violent side-slip she had experienced before.

Someone had just extinguished the candle.

The Circle was broken.

Panic threatened. She was trapped down here. She had no idea where the nearest escape route might be. She went to the door, outside a narrow, low-roofed passage, hell-lit by red-flamed braziers, curved out of sight in either direction. The walls were smooth stone and decorated with the same symbols Rebecca had seen on the stairs. There were doors, iron like hers, and tight shut.

Which way? If she made a blind guess, she could end up trapped, lost. There was a roar, screams, and then shrieks that could be Cuthella. Some sort of ambush had occurred. A fight was in progress.

She drew back into the room and slammed the door. At least if she remained in here, Elabeth and her people would know where to find her.

Wouldn't they?

Arms clutched around her midriff, Rebecca gasped for breath. The air had turned to paste. The low ceiling bore down on her. And above the ceiling, stone, soil, concrete and bricks. Such solidity, such fragility. She stumbled to the bed and sat down. She had to regain control, had to slow her breathing. It was alright. The door was shut. There was water, light. She could stay in here for several days.

In here.

Locked in and pressed in and trapped, trapped, TRAPPED.

From outside came the sounds of running feet. Rebecca tensed, muscles tight, joints aching with tension. Angry with herself for giving up so easily, she cast about for a weapon, and picked up the fork that lay on the discarded plate of curry. Not much of a weapon, but it was all she had.

The door burst open, and she surged to her feet, fork extended awkwardly.

"Are you going got eat me?" Tina asked and Rebecca's tension collapsed into a loud, high-pitched laughter that was hard to bring under control.

"Come on," Tina said. "We've got to go. There's a problem."

Drive was waiting outside, Elabeth carried in the crock of his massive, fat-soft left arm. Before she could protest, Rebecca was nestled into his right.

Tina led the way, sprinting lightly ahead. She never seemed to tire and, like Drive, never once hesitated as she negotiated the twists, turns and junctions that webbed these chambers.

"What happened to the Circle?" Rebecca asked.

"There's a traitor among us." Tina sounded only slightly breathless. "Waiting until you arrived and all the fighters were gathered together. It's a massacre."

As if cued by some Divine Director, tumult erupted some way behind them, cries and a howl of pain that turned liquid and faded to a desperate sob.

"Drive, we have to hurry," Tina urged. "The others won't be able to hold them for long."

"Sadly, yes," Drive answered and the pace quickened.

Elabeth said nothing.

The passages narrowed. The temperature dropped, the air turned damp. Time-sense disintegrated. The universe had become an ill-lit tomb, an eternity of unsteady light, rank dripping water and trapped echoes.

The passage ended.

At a wall. No door, no way through. A dead end. A trap.

"I thought you knew the way," Drive protested to Tina and sounded more offended than afraid. But Rebecca, crushed in his arm, could feel the physical thrum of his panic. "I thought you knew, you promised you knew." He was crying, Dear Jesus, the great creature was sobbing like a child.

"Oh I do," Tina said brightly. "But that isn't what I'm supposed to do tonight. Extinguish the candle and make sure Elabeth and Rebecca are taken alive. *That's* my job. I'm sorry Drive." And her receptionist's smile gleamed, even down here where a single torch spluttered out a crazed dance of light and shadows bore in from all sides.

Chapter Fourteen

The smile faded, Tina the Receptionist threw back her head and opened her mouth, then more then her mouth, wider and wider until it looked as if her entire head was torn apart. Her tongue flickered out, and out, long, longer, endlessly sliding from her throat, thicker now, no longer a tongue, but something that lashed the air, blistered by protrusions and membranous sacs.

"You wouldn't want to know what I am . . ."

Drive dropped both Rebecca and Elabeth and launched himself at what had once been Tina. Rebecca landed hard on the base of her spine. Slumped against the wall, she watched through a haze of pain as Drive grabbed at whatever was emerging from Tina's mouth. The tongue whipped out of his reach then Tina's head finally ripped itself open and her body wrenched itself inside out.

Rebecca vomited. Huddled on her hands and knees, the pain of her fall easing but her head spinning as her own stomach seemed to invert itself inside her.

Tina was now something that made no sense, a bloody, glistening fury of arms, talons and teeth, and tentacles that could have been intestines. Organs and vessels pulsed and glistened over her body, bones protruded white from the mess. She opened out, like an obscene blanket of skin to which human offal had been glued. Her reversed flesh became wings that hurled her at Drive's tiny head.

The huge man staggered back, his upper body tightly wrapped in the membrane. He hit the wall and pitched forward onto his knees. He clawed at the cloying, blood-sodden blanket, uttered a terrible gagging sound and began to convulse.

Rebecca drove herself to her feet and scrabbled weakly at the flesh-mask. It tightened, was too smooth for purchase. Rebecca shouted at Elabeth, who ignored her, who sat, head bowed and silent in the shadows. Rebecca began to pummel the Tina-thing, a desperate, tear-soaked hammering of her small fist against the drum-tight sac. Drive fell forwards. The impact was heavy and awful. His spine arced back on itself, his huge feet drummed the dank stone floor. Rebecca scratched and clawed and tried to force at least a fingernail under the ghastly, living hood.

Drive's spine wrenched itself further back than seemed possible. Something cracked. Then he collapsed and was still. Rebecca heard herself yelling and sobbing. The skin sac shrivelled under her frantic beating and tearing. There was suddenly so much blood.

Rebecca fell away, and half sat, half lay again the wall. She sobbed and gagged and rained curses down on Elabeth's unresponsive head. She was still ranting when the light appeared.

It was a dull, pulsing glow that reached round the bend in the passage they had negotiated a few minutes before. Too broken and weak to move, Rebecca waited. G'ein produced chemical light. Perhaps they were not to be taken alive after all. Well, thank God for that.

Her death was going to be painful, but not slow. She wouldn't make a beautiful corpse after those things had finished with her, but there would be no one to see her. No one would know where she had gone. She would be one of the missing. That would be hard for her parents, not knowing, never sure, hoping that she might one day turn up, and all the while her corpse would moulder and finally disintegrate in these forgotten tunnels under the very church around which they centred their lives.

How many other missing had strayed into the Place?

The light strengthened and she began to be afraid.

The glow heightened even further, too bright to be a G'ein. An army of them perhaps? Its source rounded the corner. For a moment Rebecca struggled to comprehend what it was. Then, as it came closer Rebecca understood.

Oh God no. Oh Jesus...How she understood.

She had seen this creature before, that Sunday morning in Foxhill wood when she had re-visited Dr Samuels' shallow grave then panicked and stumbled into the Place.

She pushed herself back against the wall. She began to shout, then scream Elabeth's name, and a hand found hers, across Drive's corpse. She looked up and in the last moment, illuminated by the rainbow pulsing of the great slug, saw Elabeth crawling towards her. They clutched at each other.

And hell began.

It was the relentless approach of the creature. It was its touch, the feel of it, the yielding, gelatinous texture, cold, dank. It was the press of it against her foetus-curled body. The unending pressure as it flowed over her and covered her and buried her alive under tons and tons of infinite flesh. It was the clawing, suffocating lack of air.

Then worse, it was the hole, the hot, toothless opening that drew her, that sucked her and enclosed and covered her and entombed and held and pushed and pulled and slithered over her face and stopped her mouth and nose until darkness rushed in and her head roared and she felt she would dissolve.

The tube opened out, and she slithered into a foul-smelling mush. She couldn't tell which way was up, she was drowning, clawing, thrashing. Her head broke the surface, her feet touched bottom and she managed to stand. The mush was waist deep and had the consistency of syrup. There was some light, the pulsing shifting glow of the creature's internal energies and it was enough to show her that its stomach was far from empty.

It was hung and lined with its vital organs, with vessels and things that pulsed and squeezed. The fluid in which she stood surged about her. Things bumped against her, and in the uncertain glow she saw that they were the mouldering, half digested remains of once-living things. Sightless eyes glared at her, limbs lazily drifted in to caressed her blindly then spiralled away.

She was too exhausted, too disorientated to be horrified.

Wasn't a stomach filled with vicious acids?

Then why wasn't she burning?

Perhaps the creature simply let things die of starvation and thirst, then let its food rot naturally before washing it into its system. Slow death then. Thirst would kill her first, but not for a while, not for days. She clenched her fists, bit her lip, the pain snapped off the first tremors of panic.

"Elabeth?" she whispered. Then wondered why she felt she had to be quiet. She repeated the name more loudly.

Rebecca saw a shape, indistinct, clinging to some rope of offal that looped low from the top of the creature's belly. She splashed and struggled across to her. "Is there anything we can do?" Rebecca asked. "We can't stay in here and die."

Elabeth didn't answer.

"God, don't you care? What sort of leader are you?"

Disgusted, Rebecca waded and clawed her way to the wall of the slug's maw. She pressed her hands into the cold, gelatinous flesh. Although it was translucent, she could see nothing of the outside. The slug was moving, probably back through the passageways under the chapel, perhaps burrowing underground, Rebecca had no idea.

She closed her eyes and forced herself to breathe deeply and slowly. The air was vile, it tasted of corruption, and twisted her stomach, but she had to stay calm. Could she force her way back up the creature's gullet?

Did it have a vomit reflex? She began to struggle through the murk in the direction of the creature's head. Progress was slow, the stomach floor bounced and swayed under her feet, the maw was a mass of gristly, glistening obstructions. Her feet caught on unspeakable obstacles.

It was hopeless.

No, at least she was trying, at least she had purpose. Stop fighting and she would end up with her face pressed against the skin of the slug, eyes blank, mind shattered. It had happened to Elabeth already.

The light outside changed abruptly.

She still couldn't make out any detail, but gained the impression that they had entered a building. Or was it part of the chapel complex? She had no sense of time passing, of distance. Her courage failed. This meant they were being taken to the Woman and whatever horrors she had prepared for them.

"You should have listened to Tina."

Rebecca started. Elabeth was beside her, head bowed, leaning wearily against the outer wall.

"What are you talking about?" Rebecca was shocked by the bitterness in her voice. Surely this wasn't how she was. Sweet, tolerant and forgiving, that was the real Rebecca wasn't it?

"Tina told you to trust us."

"Trust, how could she talk about trust? She betrayed -"

"She did what was necessary."

The slug lurched, seemed to be ascending. Its floor folded and rippled as if it was climbing stairs.

"What are you telling me Elabeth? That you ordered her to break the Circle? And to kill Drive?"

"The only ones who can stop this are you and I. The others had to die so we could fulfil our purpose."

"My God…My God I can't believe this. You planned for your own followers to be wiped out."

"How else could we get into the Woman's House?"

Appalled, Rebecca turned her back to the wall and averted her face from Elabeth. The slug levelled out. "There must have been a different way of doing this."

"No other. Only David knows where the Engine is and only you can do what is needed when you find it."

The Engine?

An Engine was a Machine wasn't it?

94

And some machines were crosses on which martyrs died…Rebecca remembered the stained glass images in the roof of Avy's house.

Rebecca sensed a quick movement from Elabeth and when she turned to look saw that the woman was clutching a gleaming, long-bladed knife. She flinched back. There was no longer any guarantee that the blade wasn't intended for her. All logic seemed to have fled, along with loyalties and concepts of friend and foe.

"It's time now Rebecca," Elabeth snapped, then lifted the weapon and sliced it downwards into the flesh of the slug.

The creature bucked and convulsed, throwing Rebecca backwards into the mush once more. Elabeth remained on her feet, hacking and slicing at the creature's flesh. Life fluids bubbled and ran, the foul mush in which Rebecca struggled and flailed slopped like a storm-ruffled sea.

"Now," Elabeth yelled. "Rebecca, quickly!"

Rebecca saw Elabeth force herself through the wound she had hacked into the creature's flank. Rebecca made to follow. Her limbs were stiff and awkward. Her legs gave way and she dropped face down among the dead the mouldering. Up again, a final effort, clawing and slipping until she reached the bleeding gash in the slug's side. She rammed her head through, her shoulders. The skin drew tight around her. She pushed and struggled but she was jammed. Then Elabeth was there, hauling her by the hair, her arms.

The wound gave way and Rebecca poured out and onto the floor, where she lay in a pool of gore. She wanted to stay there and never move again. She didn't care about the filth she wallowed in. She was tired, confused, lost.

There was a terrible burning smell, a thin veil of orange smoke, and voices. A discordant choir that uttered a terrible, terrible moaning.

Rebecca sat up, blinked and tried to comprehend what she saw.

They were in a passage, bright-lit though the light was uncertain. The ceiling was high, arched and like the walls, white. It was, however, the alcoves that sucked her attention. She stared at them, fascinated then appalled when she comprehended what they contained. A fire burned in each one, the source of the illumination. Each conflagration was wrapped about a figure, its fuel Rebecca supposed. But then she saw that the figures were moving, writhing, and howling with pain.

None of them was human.

All were Cast-Outs, the bizarre and hulking and beautiful.

Burning alive. Oh God, burning…

Rebecca stumbled towards the nearest alcove, possessed of some vague, panic-forged idea of helping the rotund, squat goblin-like thing it contained. It stared at her, mouth open, flesh blistered and molten. Its eyes held no sanity.

The fire didn't change. The goblin's agony neither increased for diminished. It was eternal. The way Hell was eternal.

She really was in Hell. She had been right on that Sunday evening when the idea had occurred to her that she might well already be suffering her everlasting damnation. But her punishment seemed to be less than these poor wretches endured. Oh God, it was unthinkable. She stopped, kept at bay by the heat and the stench.

"You can help them," Elabeth said, quietly, even gently.

"We need something to douse the -"

"Not here," Elabeth answered. She touched Rebecca's shoulder, translating spoke gentleness into the physical. "The Engine is the key."

"I don't understand." She couldn't look away from the fire and the creature that writhed and shrieked inside it. Then, suddenly, she was angry. "I don't bloody understand!" Her rage finally tore her round to face Elabeth.

The view was no better, something that twisted and flapped fire-ruined wings burned beyond Elabeth's shoulder. The heat was immense, the oily smoke clawed at Rebecca's throat, weighed on her lungs.

"No more riddles, okay? No more stupid fucking puzzles and stupid fucking games. What *is* this Engine?"

"The soul, the heart."

Rebecca closed her smoke stung eyes. "Is that what would have happened to us?" She said. "Would we have ended up in one of those alcoves?"

"Or something similar. The Cast Outs fuels more than the P's lamps."

Elabeth held Rebecca's shoulders again. Rebecca opened her eyes and stared back at her. "You are dangerous to them. They're terrified of you Rebecca. You are The Woman and they don't want you anywhere near The Engine."

"No," Rebecca backed away. "No, Bezzec told me I was the *same* as the Woman. That I was a Changeling..." Only Bezzec had never mentioned Changelings had he. *She* had assumed that it to be the case.

Only David spoken of Changelings, and only David had disregarded the Sajanath. The realisation disturbed her.

"The People want the Engine to remain as it is because that means everything else will stay as it is. David wants the Engine destroyed, because that will bring an end the People' power, this house will fall, the Cast-Outs and their Liberator will be free. But there is another alternative. And *that* will be up to you Rebecca."

Abruptly Elabeth set off down the corridor. She blurred quickly into the smoke. Trying to ignore the fires, hand over her mouth as if that would somehow keep the stink from her lungs, Rebecca followed. She glanced behind, caught a last glimpse of the quivering wreckage of the slug.

Oh yes, she mused. There is another alternative. She had seen it, stain-glassed across the roof of Avy's house. Surely not...Oh God, not that. Mechanical crucifixion, martyrdom was something Rebecca Ann Samuels could never contemplate.

She heard something, loud enough to separate it from the crackle and moan. Her mouth dried, if the Cuthella appeared now then they wouldn't stand a chance. Another backward glance showed nothing. She coughed, gagged on the roasting flesh stink. She had smelled this before, in her garden, the first time a Cuthella had attacked her.

More noise. Rebecca moved closer to Elabeth and found some comfort in her proximity.

A roar.

Elabeth grabbed her hand and they ran. Louder, closer. She turned, she couldn't help it, and saw, heads, four, five, rushing towards her, vaguely human, white-fleshed, mouths open, too far. Their necks stretched away into the smoke behind them, serpentine, as pallid-fleshed as the heads they bore.

Stretching, towards.

Her.

Closer.

Close.

She smelled their breath, rotten fruit stink.

Elabeth halted and spun round. Rebecca swerved to avoid her and almost crashed into one of the fires. She rebounded off the wall beside it, felt a momentary give in the wall's surface, a felt the warmth, like living flesh. Then there was no more time for shock or revulsion. The heads erupted at them. Rebecca cowered back, waited for the pain.

Elabeth raised her arms, held them open, a martyr's pose.

The first of the heads thrust towards Elabeth.

And flinched back.

The others did the same, their rush halted, hovering at the end of their long, pallid necks. Their red eyes were fear-wide. *Fear*-wide. Rebecca realised that they were afraid of Elabeth.

Rebecca saw the ripple shudder through Elabeth's torso.

The heads drew back, slowly.

Elabeth lowered her arms.

"It isn't time yet," she said simply, then walked again.

The corridor seemed endless, a gentle curve into infinity. And always, there were the living torches, the smoke and the cries.

The ceiling bulged.

Rebecca almost stopped, but pressed on, passed under the protrusion. A moment later she was startled by a dull thud behind her and when she turned, she saw a Cuthella. It appeared to struggle, to twist and thrash, as if escaping from some sort of binding. Another dropped in front of them and Rebecca saw that the binding was a glistening, transparent sac, like a birth sac.

Rebecca screamed, in fear, a warning to Elabeth, who took Rebecca's hand and hauled her towards the Cuthella that barred their way. The creature, free of its cocoon, cowered at Elabeth's passing, but followed at a distance as soon as she and Rebecca were clear of it.

More appeared, some already born – the only way Rebecca could think of their arrival – others squeezed from the walls or dropped from the ceiling.

All of them shrank from Elabeth as she passed by.

There were Ge'in too. They oozed from shadowed corners, but recoiled from the nearness of Elabeth. When Rebecca glanced behind, she saw the heads again, following on their seemingly endless necks. None of the horrors that stalked the two women, came closer than ten feet.

The corridor ended at a door.

Guarded by a handful of Cuthella, fresh born and mucus dripping.

Still towing Rebecca by the hand, Elabeth, didn't hesitate. As before, the Cuthella stirred uneasily, then melted apart and crushed themselves against the walls to allow the two women entry.

Elabeth pushed at the door, which was grand, arched and made of the same fibrous material as the gantries in Avy's house. It opened, not only unlocked, but not properly closed. Elabeth stood aside to allow Rebecca access. Rebecca glanced back along the smoke-veiled corridor. "I'll help you," she whispered, then stepped through.

She saw David and screamed his name.

Chapter Fifteen

He hung, naked and upside down, from a thick rope. His arms were twisted up behind him, his wrists bound in a contortion that looked like a reversed prayer. As he rotated slowly and endlessly, Rebecca was shown his face and saw the disfigurement of agony.

The rope was fixed to a point infinitely high in a vast, vaulted ceiling. As she stumbled into the room, Rebecca saw that the rope was not rope at all, but organic, something like a huge, purple-red umbilical. The chamber itself was flesh. Its walls, floor, roof and the pillars that supported it, all formed from tangled, living Cast-Out bodies.

Their faces, like David's were contorted into masks of pain.

They sighed, the sound like the cry of a grief-struck wind.

"Let him go," Rebecca whispered. "Let him go. LET HIM GO!"

Her voice snapped across the room. The Cast-Out sighs grew loud, then faded.

We can't let you have him, the sigh told her. The voice was that of the Cast-Outs, but not theirs. Something lay behind it, something powerful, yet petulant.

Something familiar.

"Please —" Rebecca stopped herself, squared her shoulders and dared to shout; "I am The Woman, and I order you to release him." She felt her cheeks burn as soon as the words were out. It sounded ridiculous, even here in this bizarre Heaven-Hell.

You don't understand. If we let you have him then this will all end.

"It has to end," Rebecca said quietly. "All this cruelty..." Words tangled then dried. Rebecca Ann Samuels wasn't given to making speeches.

She became aware that the Cuthella who followed them into the chamber were slowly arcing about her on either side the way an amoeba surrounds its microscopic prey. Rebecca felt too weak to fight.

Cruelty? No Rebecca, purity, bought with blood.

Bewildered, Rebecca took a step back. The only blood-deal she knew of was the one Pastor Emerson had taught her, the sacrifice of Christ.

"Whose blood?" she asked. Did it matter, she was in trouble. The Cuthella had all but surrounded her, an impenetrable wall of malevolent, violent flesh. The Cuthella were at the door. David was in

99

agony and beyond her reach.

Why David's of course. His blood created this.

So he was a martyr as well.

We love him. We want him and we're going to keep him.

Arms reached out, lengthened and distorted into tendrils that caressed David's taut, flesh.

"If you love him so much, why don't you untie him?" Rebecca said.

And the Cuthella surged in. Rebecca watched them come, more fascinated than afraid. There was no hope or escape, there was no choice but to resign herself.

Elabeth moved, swept the knife from the folds of her dress.

One knife?

Against this many?

Elabeth raised the weapon. She looked at Rebecca, her face ashen, and torn with grief. "Time now," she whispered.

And the knife arced downwards and inwards.

Coward, Rebecca screamed silently at the woman as the blade sliced through her muck-spattered, Edwardian dress. Blood flowed, and Rebecca's anger blanked into white horror. Elabeth's face was impassive, her eyes wide. But she didn't cry out. Instead she ripped the knife upwards from her belly to her chest.

Things poured out.

Not entrails though, birds. No, not birds, something more terrible, sharp-clawed, razor-billed…

Sometime later, when it was over, Rebecca, who had dropped onto her haunches and covered her head with her arms, looked up and saw Elabeth lying on the floor next to her. The woman's mouth and eyes were wide, her body an empty cage. Next, she saw Elabeth's children, who covered the chamber floor, gorging themselves on the scattered corpses of the Cuthella they had overwhelmed and slaughtered.

David lay on the floor, his arms still bound. Presumably the birds had cut – or bitten – David free. Rebecca crawled over and helped David into a sitting position. He was breathing hard, weak.

"The Engine…" he rasped.

No, please. . .

Rebecca cast about and saw Elabeth's knife. She prised the blade from her hand then sawed at the tissue binding David's wrists. Once free, he moved his arms slowly, grimacing with pain.

We've waited so long.

"Where is this engine?" Rebecca asked.

"We go together."

"But you're too weak —"

"We go together. Help me up."

David. . .

Rebecca struggled David up onto his feet. He stood, stared about the chamber.

David, don't do this, our love, please...

"Don't listen to them," Rebecca's voice was hoarse. "We have to get to the Engine." Listen to her, an expert on all things Place now wasn't she.

David seemed to shake himself, nodded. "I'm sorry," he murmured and Rebecca wasn't sure whether it was for her or for the P.

They crossed to the door. The birds who were feasting, stirred and some flew on ahead, returned, and flew on again. Their escort.

David. . .

The cry tore at Rebecca's heart. David hesitated, his face haggard with grief as well as pain, then pushed on into the corridor.

Which was full of Cuthella, crouched in the smoke, their flesh painted with flame. The birds chattered and darted, the Cuthella drew back.

As they walked, rounding that everlasting curve, Rebecca noticed that even though scores perhaps hundreds of Cuthella were being born here, many were weak, or deformed, short of limbs, jaws moulded together, eyeless. They mewled and squealed, pathetic enough to evince something like sympathy from her.

The temperature dropped.

Rebecca's breath was now puffs of condensation.

One of the birds dropped to the floor. It convulsed then was still.

The death of the creature sent a ripple through the Cuthella. Those that were disabled writhed and snarled.

Another bird died.

Rebecca glanced at David who was looking stronger, but detached. Suddenly this David was a stranger and it angered her. She had risked her life for him and he had lied to her, about the Sajanath, about Changelings.

More birds died.

A howl echoed down the passage way from behind them. Rebecca looked back and saw that the Cuthella were following more boldly. The surviving birds darted at them.

David's hand tightened about hers.

More birds died.

"There, see it, the exit."

Rebecca looked ahead, and saw a square of light.

"Run," David said quietly. "Now. *Run.*"

He yanked at her hand and powered towards the light. His strength was immense and what he had called his skills, intact, because, suddenly, he scuttered up the side of the tunnel and, with Rebecca in tow, ran along the ceiling, upside-down, up-side-bloody-fucking-down.

Oh how she loved swearing.

She heard them then, the massed shriek of the Cuthella. She closed her eyes and let David take her. They were under her head, obscured by smoke from which their claws lashed and kissed her hair.

I'm going to save you, she whispered to the Cast-Outs who writhed and burned below her.

Rebecca tried to gain a purchase but David was too fast, her feet left the ground – ceiling - and trailed behind her.

The air changed.

Became cold and dank.

David slowed, spiralled down to the floor once more and Rebecca saw that they were jogging along damp, loamy ground. Trees, or something like them, bowed over their heads, so low they were forced to crouch as they ran. The light was pond-green, the air thick and foul-smelling.

She glanced down and saw that with every foot fall, black, stinking moisture was squeezed out onto the mossy soil. Things wriggled and squirmed, some many-legged, others huge, flesh-coloured worms.

"Are we out of the House?" Rebecca asked.

"There isn't such thing as in or out," David answered.

"I…" Don't understand? Of course she didn't. "Why don't the Cuthella follow us?"

"Because they don't need to."

Oh, wonderful, frying pans and fires sprang to Rebecca's mind. She realised that this too was a passage, just like the one in the House.

Shivering, she clutched at David's hand. Her jaw stiffened her teeth clattered. Branches slashed at her hair, she cried out and ducked lower. More branches brushed her arms. The passage was turning into a tunnel. Her feet sank deeper into the miry floor. The stink was unbearable. The worms were all over her, crawling up her legs, clinging to her flesh with minute and sharp teeth. Their heads…Jesus, their tiny heads were human, old man faces.

She wanted to brush them away but David wouldn't let her.

The branches were in her face, they forced her onto her hands and knees, hands sinking into the mire, crushing worms, while others oozed out and over her flesh. Scuttling things dropped for the roof, over her neck, in her hair, down her dress.

Finally, she was forced onto her belly, she could just see the soles of David's feet as he led her deeper into the tunnel. She slithered through worms, hardly more than a nematode herself.

She was bitten, scratched, invaded.

She was slithering into an impossible space where it was dark, wet and stinking.

She wanted to get out.

David broke through first, she followed and it was bright and dry. She dropped onto grass, lay there and felt the sun shrivel the crawling and slithering things. Eyes closed, she wasn't interested in where she was.

Her eyes were still closed when David kissed her.

The kiss was deep and warm. The kiss opened her and she pulled him down on top of her. Her hands slid about his back and she felt the hot, dryness of his skin. His weight burrowed into her and she was lost in the dark, alone with David, in her room, deep into the silent hours. She cried as she clawed at him and crushed him down onto and into her. He murmured her name, at first, a whisper, then a moan, a shout.

There's only you Rebecca. . .

A wave gathered, rose and crashed down through her.

She opened her eyes.

And saw that they were lying in the ancient graveyard behind Abbotsfield Baptist chapel. A tilted, moss-infested slab provided concealment. The gravestone commemorated some long-forgotten patriarch named Eleazer Smith who fell asleep in Jesus in 1876.

High above, a lark warbled its endless cyclical song. The sky disappeared, replaced by David's face. He kissed Rebecca's forehead.

She sighed, reached up and drew him down onto herself once more. His arms slid about her and she rested in his embrace.

"I knew you would come for me," he murmured.

"Let's go –" Home? Was that what she had been about to say? Home, where Detective Inspector March would be waiting. Rebecca had forgotten, for a moment. The corpse they had found in Foxhill

Wood would have to remain unidentified, but the police must have found a treasure strove of forensic evidence linking her to it by now; her fingerprints all over the body, fibres and skin flakes in the boot of the BMW.

"There are a million places we can go," David said. Was that places or Places? "But first we have to destroy the Engine."

"Do we have to go back into the House?" Dear God, she couldn't go back there –

"No," David answered gently. "The Engine is here."

Rebecca pulled away. "Here?"

David nodded towards the chapel. "In there."

"The chapel? Why didn't Elabeth's band destroy it? They've been hiding right beside it for God knows how long."

"They didn't know it was there. And only you can destroy it Rebecca."

"Me…" Another realisation. Another puzzle. "Because I'm The Woman. Is that it?" She was exasperated now. Talking too loudly. She sighed and dropped her voice back to a whisper. "Elabeth said there was another alternative. She said that the People wanted it to remain as it is, that you want it destroyed because it will bring down the People and set the Cast-Outs, and you, free. But she said there's a third choice, *my* choice. What is it David?"

"You don't have to take that path -"

"What happens if I do?"

"Hell comes back."

"I saw a picture, in Avy's home…"

"Hell comes back Rebecca. Do you want that? Hell for both of us."

"What Hell? And what about the others, the People and the Cast-Outs? Do they suffer this Hell?"

"This universe is yours Rebecca. We all have one."

"But I'm not a dictator. You're the Liberator, that's what Bezzec and Elabeth told me. You were fighting against the Woman."

"No, what the Woman has *become*. Cause and effect Rebecca, butterfly wings. What occurs in one place affects another."

That made no sense. Unless… "What I've *become*?"

There's only you Rebecca.

The sentence speared into her. David had cried it out a moment before, when they made love. The way Dr David Samuels used to cry it out in the quiet dark, on those good times, when love had shown through the cracks in the pain.

"Are there such things as Changelings David? Is there only *one* David Samuels?

No answer. In a moment he was on his feet and, crouched low, running towards the rear of the chapel. Rebecca followed, wondering what other choice had?

The sound of the big arched chapel window breaking was like an explosion in the early morning silence of the village. It brought the sound of a police siren. There was no shortage of police in Abbotsfield at the moment.

Rebecca placed her foot in David's cupped hands then heaved herself through the glass-fanged hole that led into the chapel. She wanted to question him, but there was suddenly no time because the police were coming and David was her only hope.

She cut her hand, tore her dress and gashed her right calf. The drop was cumbersome. She almost fell, but managed to land on her feet. The police siren was close now. Breathing hard, trying to ignore the pain of her injuries and the crashing of her heart, Rebecca turned to help David. He was framed in the shattered window then he jumped. Somehow, despite being naked, he managed to avoid cutting himself. Rebecca wanted his arms again, but hesitated, her feelings too confused.

Is there only one David Samuels?

Without a word, he strode past her to the front of the chapel then wrenched at the front pew.

It tipped easily, and crashed deafeningly onto its neighbour behind.

"Give me hand," he said. Rebecca went to him, dropped to her knees and clawed at the loose floorboards below. She had to help him. She had nowhere else to go and no one else to turn to. And he loved her.

He was, after all, David.

A police car skidded to a halt outside. There were shouts, radio crackle.

A second floorboard, a thud-thud, voices.

Fists on the chapel door. Shouts.

A third floorboard.

Now a shout from outside the broken window.

The fourth floorboard. A gap. David dropped into the darkness first.

Head and shoulders appeared in the window frame. More radio-crackle, louder then before. A grunt of effort.

Rebecca squeezed herself into the gap, her sweater caught on a wood splinter, trapped her then ripped free.

"David?" Rebecca whispered in the black. "Where are you?"

She started as his hand closed around hers and pulled. Boots were stomping the floor above her head. It wouldn't be long before a police officer dropped into the dark behind her.

There was enough light from the torn up floorboards to grey the dark and outline David. He was barging at a door. She heard the thud of his bare shoulder as it slammed against wood.

Rebecca made to got to him, but stumbled over some object and fell against the nearest wall. It took a moment for her to understand that the wall was formed by the sheer side of the baptism pool. She had been submerged in its tepid water one sunny Sunday evening, twenty or so yeas ago, and had emerged as a brand new, dripping wet believer for Pastor Emerson to add to his flock. The congregation had sung "Praise the Lord".

Her eyes adjusted to the gloom, and she saw that the object she had tripped over was a hammer, one of a handful of discarded tools, scattered over the floor, presumably long forgotten by the workmen who had constructed the baptism pool. There was a brace and bit, a screwdriver with a bulbous wooden handle.

A hammer.

She grabbed it, not knowing why and frightened by the way it sat in her hand, so familiar, so *right*. Someone ripped at floorboards above their heads. Startled, Rebecca hissed David's name. He didn't reply or even turn to her but slumped against the door. He was breathing hard. Rebecca hurried over to him, kicking discarded tools aside as she did so. She touched his shoulder.

"Use this," Rebecca said and passed the hammer to David. He pushed himself from the door, weighed the tool in his hand, seemed to regain some strength from its touch and began pounding it at the door. The noise was deafening.

A figure dropped to the floor behind her.

"Stop –"

There was a splintering sound. David snapped Rebecca's name and she followed as he pushed open the door.

To reveal the Engine.

Which illuminated its shaft-shaped chamber with fires and lightning-blue electric arcs.

The Engine was vast. When Rebecca looked up she couldn't see its summit and sensed that it had none, but was rammed through countless layers of sky and universe. It had no lateral borders either but grew from the walls, moulded from the masonry, brick turning to iron, to flesh-textured pipes and vessels, to mucus-dripping cables.

The Engine was terrible.

It was iron and vast cogs and chains and boilers that spewed flame and smoke, and was perfumed with oil and steam. Pistons rammed in and out of casings with terrifying force. There was something alive about it. And discordant. The engine rattled and clanged and was picking up speed even as Rebecca watched. It was out of control, malfunctioning.

It bore down and oppressed.

Drew.

"Fucking hell."

Rebecca turned and saw a police officer framed in the doorway. He was partially obscured by David.

"Take this, Rebecca," he said and threw the hammer towards her. "You know how to use it."

He ignored the police officer, who seemed too awestruck to act.

Rebecca missed the hammer, she never was good at sport, and it clattered onto the floor. Rebecca stared at it for a moment then picked it up. The floor seemed to ripple upwards at her touch, like a caress, a kiss. Despite The Engine's discordant roar and rage, she felt no fear.

This was *her* room.

The hammer handle was gritty and she could feel the oil ground into its wood. She shivered. Then she turned back to The Engine and wondered how the hell she could break it with such a pitiful tool.

"What do I do?" she said.

"Go closer and you'll see." His words were clear, as if through rather than above the din.

"Help me David."

"I can't, it won't let anyone near it but you."

Again, that god-like status she seemed to have attained.

"Because I'm The Woman?"

His silence was yes.

She moved, slowly, warily as if stalking a wild and dangerous beast. Its mechanisms speeded up as she approached, a storm of vibration and discordant machineries.

Then she saw the orb.

It was set deep into the machine's trunk, behind the thrashing pistons and whirling wheels. It seemed of little consequence, little

107

larger than a skull, clear and housing nothing more than a flickering, blue-white arc.

But that was the machine's heart, its centre, its soul, fragile, vulnerable.

Easily shattered with a single blow.

Rebecca moved closer. The machine bore down on her, its vibration tremoring through the hard paved floor. She lifted the hammer slightly. The machine stepped up to even greater frenzy. She recoiled, sure the titanic thing was about to shatter in a flesh-annihilating holocaust of boiling oil and splintered iron.

She stopped.

There was something else, an aperture, moulded into the trunk below the orb. As she stared she saw that it resembled a human figure, arms outstretched, crucifixion-wise.

I'm not supposed to destroy it.

Because there is only you Rebecca

And only *you* David.

No Changelings, that was a story, told to her to keep it simple…

Only one.

"No Rebecca." David was pleading now. She turned back to see him. He stood, naked, head bowed, all his strength gone, vulnerable and afraid. She had seen this before. Many, many times.

She had seen *David* like this.

"I have to go in there don't I. just like the picture in the stain glass window."

"… bring Hell back…"

Back? So she had been there before. They had *both* been there before, her and David.

"Why does it feel like the other David when you make love to me? Are you… are you part of him? Is that it?"

The part I love. The part I want, the one I set free when I…

She turned, saw David, flanked now by three police officers, and a woman in a coat and trouser suit, Detective Inspector Sue March. All of them were too transfixed to make any move.

Rebecca stared at David, aching to go back to this perfect man, without the weakness, the vulnerability, the humanity of the man she had loved.

Then she ran to the machine. March called out for her to stop.

The killing tornado of iron and flame parted at her approach and she was inside the pumping, spinning, roaring madness of the machine. There were pipes, like the gantries and branches in Avy's house. She began to climb, difficult with a hammer in her hand.

She reached the moulding quickly. Above, within arms reach was the fragile, fragile orb.

Rebecca clung to a hot oily pipe and raised the hammer. Freedom was a hammer blow away. She clenched the hammer, tightly, brought her arm back over her shoulder.

Heard David shout encouragement.

One blow and he was hers that was it wasn't it.

There's only you Rebecca.

…*"There is only you Rebecca," he would say in that same quiet voice. She would make him love her then, in those rare, small hours moments. That was when their loving flared bright and true and needed no erotic artifice to stay its course.*

Brief moments then, soon lost.

Rebecca opened her hand and felt the hammer fall away.

David's howl of despair was lost in the Engine's throb and rage.

Rebecca swung round and shuffled herself into the moulding. No, she shouldn't do this… She saw him, run forward, scoop up the hammer, hurl it upwards for her to catch. Up it came, oh up and up, arcing slowly, slowly, guided towards her outstretched fingers by the same skills that had healed poor old Elizabeth Etheridge's arthritis-crippled back

Its handle brushed her fingertips then fell away.

As

She pushed herself back into the moulding and flung her arms outwards into their crucifix slots.

The pain was immense as tube and iron were plunged into her flesh, she felt herself tear and burn. The pain became red. She was ripped apart.

Chapter Sixteen

This time there was a hammer in her hand.

It was a claw hammer, its handle oil-stained, its head resembling some crested bird or dinosaur. There was a certain, comfortable weight to the tool. And a madness that seethed like electricity at the meeting of flesh and grease-grained wood.

Her husband was turning away from the gleaming bulk of the old Humber that was his toy, his first love, his *project*. Turning back towards *her*, enraged because she had followed him through the house and into the garage, *his* garage, pleading for some dignity, for some respect, for him simply to talk about it.

Her husband's body twisted about like a slow motion film of a dog shaking itself dry after a swim in some icy river; first the head, then torso, then waist.

His fists were clenched.

Dear God, Dear Christ, his fists. How well she knew his fists, how often she had daubed them with bloody kisses.

This time, however, there was a hammer in her hand...

"I saw the photograph," she said.

"What photograph?" he seemed to stumble, as if tripped physically by her words. His eyes burned, though, still dangerous.

"The one in your wallet, the one of me. And you read my Bible, don't you."

Some of him, some of *her* David broke through like sun through cloud as he unclenched his fists.

"David. You've hurt me, you've humiliated me. I don't really understand why. But I don't think it's because you hate me."

"Are you leaving me, is that it?" He bowed his head, as if all his strength was gone and he was left vulnerable and afraid.

"I might. It depends." Rebecca became aware of the hammer. She opened her hand and the tool clang-thudded onto the floor. "What ever happens, you will never hit me again."

Then, on an impulse, Rebecca pulled off her overlarge woollen v-neck and the summer dress it hid. She stood, naked, vulnerable and shivering in the uncompromising iron, concrete and oil solidity of the garage. Rebecca paused for a moment then turned her back on her husband. She paused at the door that would take her back into the kitchen.

She glimpsed the wounds then, the scars on the back of her hand, like stings, the gash in her calf, and the puncture holes in her arms and all over her torso, glimpsed, then hidden from her view, like a Place that exists right there, yet unseen…

"I'll be upstairs David. It's up to you."

TPB

"Terry thinks he can sing because no one boos him when he does his turn at the local Jam Nite. *He plays harmonica as well and, as a college lecturer, tries to turn recalcitrant students into electricians. Oh, and he writes. Published in the likes of* Nemonymous, Midnight Street, Murky Depths, New Horizons *and* Bare Bone, *Terry has also written and directed three of his own plays, started up the very occasional Exaggerated Press and brought out a collection of his short fiction called* The Exaggerated Man *(available from Amazon). His novel* Bloody War *will be published by Eibonvale at the end of 2010. He is married to the poet Jessica Lawrence author of* Dreams of Flight *and* Ravaging the Urban Wildscape.*"*

Coming Soon from
www.pendragonpress.net

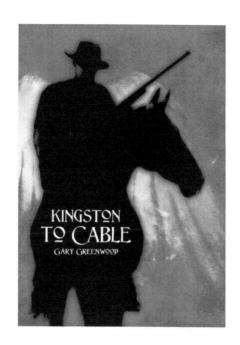